T0367933

The
Ironware
Store

WILLIAM STANLEY

ARCHWAY
PUBLISHING

Archway Publishing books may be ordered
through booksellers or by contacting:

Archway Publishing
1663 Liberty Drive
Bloomington, IN 47403
www.archwaypublishing.com
844-669-3957

ISBN: 978-1-6657-6477-3 (sc)
ISBN: 978-1-6657-6478-0 (e)

Library of Congress Control Number: 2024916921

Print information available on the last page.

Archway Publishing rev. date: 08/30/2024

DEDICATION

This book is dedicated to all who have faced adversities and have worked hard to overcome them.

CHAPTER ONE

The warm May sunshine melted the ice on the Yukon River. Paddle wheelers, along with riverboats, plied the river in the late spring, bringing supplies to Dawson in the Yukon Territory. One paddleboat was pushing an exceptionally large barge, which was fully loaded with ironware products manufactured by, and shipped from, a foundry near Portland, Oregon. These products were in big demand in the growing city of Dawson.

The barge was carrying stock for an ironware store, Samuel's Cast Iron Creations, which an entrepreneur had built and opened last summer. The products sold there were so popular, he had sold out of the contents from two previous shipments within days of receiving them. Not having anything left in his store to sell in the fall, Samuel had travelled to Seattle to spend the winter. While there, Samuel and his brother, Dave, had travelled to the foundry near Portland, Oregon and ordered the equivalent of two barge loads of goods from the company. The first part of that order was being delivered now, in late spring, with the remaining items being shipped in the latter part of summer.

Samuel had met the first load of his goods in Whitehorse and was accompanying the barge on its four-hundred-mile journey up the Yukon River to Dawson. The trip from Whitehorse was long, boring, and dangerous. The river currents were strong and large pieces of debris, washed from the shorelines, were floating in the water, creating navigational hazards. Hitting a stump or a large tree in the river could damage, or even sink, a boat. If this were to happen, there was little chance a man could survive in the currents of the mighty Yukon.

The paddleboat, with its wheel churning, rounded a corner on the river. A hundred yards in front of the boat, was the dock where they would be putting in. The captain of the paddle wheeler yelled for his crew to get ready to dock the boat. A flurry of activity signalled they were ready to assist with the difficult maneuvers the captain needed to make. The paddleboat and barge needed to be safely guided into their proper spaces along the docks. The dockhands on shore, along with the deckhands, were able to successfully dock the vessels, securing the crafts without damaging the docks.

Samuel was the first passenger to depart the paddle wheeler. His return trip to Dawson from his winter home in Seattle had been long and difficult, with little food to eat. He would be glad to return to his house in Dawson, which he had not seen since the fall. He met with the dockmaster, who told Samuel the barge needed to be emptied within three days. Samuel told the man they would begin working on that task in the morning, as he planned to hire the same company who had moved his goods from the barge to his store last year. The dockmaster assured Samuel the company was still in business, which was good to hear.

Before going home, Sam decided to visit Wendy and Jason,

good friends of his who lived a short walk from Dawson. He was hoping Wendy would offer to feed him while he was there, as he knew Wendy always had food available for unexpected company or starving individuals sent to her home for food. As Samuel approached the front door, he was greeted by Jason's dog, King, barking loudly. This made Samuel miss his own dog, Spearmint, who had been living with a neighbour in Dawson while Sam was in Seattle for the winter.

Jason opened the door to a smiling Samuel, the men embracing, glad to see each other. Jason invited his friend into the house, who was immediately hugged by Wendy. The couple's son, Kuzih, was also elated to see his friend, Samuel, climbing onto his lap the moment he sat down. Wendy offered to cook some food for Samuel, knowing he must be hungry. Luckily, a constable from the Dawson office of the North West Mounted Police had dropped off a deer he had shot yesterday. He had asked the couple to take what they needed and share the remaining meat with any Indigenous families who needed help securing food.

Soon, Samuel filled his hungry stomach with venison Wendy had prepared for him. After eating his fill, he graciously thanked the couple for their hospitality and got up from the table to walk home. He asked Wendy and Jason if they would like to work for him tomorrow at the store, helping to unload goods and place the merchandise where it belonged. The couple agreed to meet Samuel at his store at noon. Heading to the movers, who he hoped to have on the job early in the morning, Samuel wished Wendy and Jason goodbye, telling them he would see them tomorrow.

CHAPTER TWO

S amuel left Wendy and Jason's house with a full stomach. It was a short walk to the moving business, which Sam was hoping to hire to work for him tomorrow. Upon arriving, he noticed the owner, whom he had met last year, working on the wheel of one of his large wagons. Samuel approached the man, introducing himself again as the owner of the ironware store. Phil, the owner of the moving company, remembered Samuel, having moved goods for him twice from the dock to the store. Phil gladly accepted Samuel's job, telling him he would be at the dock in Dawson at 8 a.m. the following morning, along with his crew who would be ready to work.

Samuel left Phil's business a happy man. Before heading home, he had one very important stop to make, picking up his dog, Spearmint, from his neighbour's house. Samuel's dog had stayed with Ed, his trusted friend and neighbour, for the winter while Sam was in Seattle. Arriving at Ed's house, Samuel knocked on the front door and was immediately greeted by a loud bark. Ed answered the door with Spearmint standing behind him. Upon seeing who the visitor was, the dog ran past Ed and tried to jump into

Samuel's arms, knocking him to the ground. The happy dog jumped on top of him, tail wagging, licking his face with his big wet tongue. Samuel hugged Spearmint, equally as glad to see him.

Thanking Ed for watching Spearmint, Sam told him to come to the grand reopening sale at his store. Samuel had promised Ed to pay him in merchandise for taking care of his dog all winter, a deal Ed was more than pleased with. Saying goodbye to Ed, Sam and Spearmint walked the short distance home. Upon entering the house, Sam noticed the air inside smelled musty. He opened the windows of the small house and lit a fire in the woodstove he had installed last fall. Within a short time, the house was cozy, the unsavory odor disappearing.

Samuel closed the windows, as the night air was chilly for this late in the spring. He was delighted to be home, especially after the rather unpleasant trip on the paddle wheeler which carried him and his cargo here. Looking forward to sleeping in his own bed, with Spearmint on the floor beside him, Samuel went to bed, anxious about tomorrow. He hoped Phil was right when he had said his workers could move everything off the barge in one day. He had told Samuel he would have an additional wagon and crew on site this year, to ensure the work being completed. With that last thought in mind, Samuel drifted off to sleep beside his snoring dog, who was glad to be home.

CHAPTER THREE

Wendy and Jason awoke to the birds' song entering through their open bedroom window. Jason noticed the outside air was cold, retrieving another blanket from the cupboard to cover himself and Wendy. The sun was just rising over the horizon, signalling the start of another bright, sunny day. Jason and Wendy were going to Samuel's store at noon, to help him with the goods arriving at the store. After cuddling under the warm blankets for an hour, the couple pulled themselves out of bed. Jason let a waiting King outside for his morning ritual, lit a fire in the woodstove, and put the kettle on to boil. The couple had decided to walk on the trail which encircled the lake on their property after breakfast. Working hard last year, they had finished clearing the path around the water. They had plenty of time to enjoy their hike before heading to Samuel's store.

The day was sunny and warm, when the family and their dog, King, left the house. King bounded ahead, chasing his favorite rodents, the squirrels. Wendy, Jason, and Kuzih walked on, losing sight of King in the underbrush. Thirty minutes went by, when the dog's sudden barking caught their attention. This barking was followed by two deer running toward them on the trail. After seeing the couple, the animals veered off the trail, disappearing into the forest.

King returned, panting and out of breath from chasing the deer. He walked beside Wendy, Jason, and Kuzih until they returned home, where a surprise was waiting on the porch. Joe and Mary, friends of the couple who lived a few hours away, had arrived for a visit while they were on their hike. They told Wendy and Jason they had come to see if Samuel had returned from Seattle. The couple hoped he had restocked and opened his store. Joe and Mary were surprised when Wendy told them they were going to the store at noon to help Sam unload his merchandise. Joe offered to help them, while Mary offered to watch Kuzih until they finished their work. Wendy loved that idea, as it would be difficult to keep Kuzih entertained while trying to get things done.

When the helpers arrived at the store, they were greeted by Samuel, who has happy to accept Joe's help. The activity around Samuel's store attracted a large crowd of onlookers, watching the wagons come and go. They wondered when Samuel was going to reopen his store for business, anxious to inspect the new merchandise.

By 5 p.m., the barge had been emptied and all of the shipment had been placed inside the building. Wendy and Jason promised to return tomorrow, to help finish placing the merchandise in its rightful place in the store. With a sense of accomplishment, the group said goodbye and headed home to a waiting Mary and Kuzih. The trio stopped at the home of an Indigenous couple, who sold fresh and smoked fish caught from the tributaries of the Yukon River. This was Wendy and Jason's wilderness version of fast-food dining, a first for the north.

CHAPTER FOUR

Rusty, Joe and Mary's dog, and King were snoozing by the woodstove. Mary had kept a low fire burning in the stove to keep the chill out of the house. When the trio returned home from Samuel's store, everyone shared the smoked fish they had purchased for dinner. Joe and Mary planned to spend two more nights with Wendy and Jason before returning home.

Jason and Joe went outside to feed the sled dogs and the animals in the barn, while Wendy and Mary cleaned up the kitchen. The evening sky was darkening as the men finished their work. They returned to the house, joining their wives in the living room for coffee and conversation. Wendy and Jason would return to the ironware store tomorrow morning to help Samuel finish setting up his wares. Joe and Mary would come to the store after lunch with Kuzih. They wanted to shop for new merchandise for their cabin and planned to borrow Omar, one of the donkeys in the shed, to carry their purchases back to Wendy and Jason's house.

With the plan for tomorrow ironed out, the couples retired to their bedrooms, Wendy taking her cranky child, who had stayed up too late, with her. Wendy lay Kuzih down on his bed and within minutes he was sleeping. Returning to her own room, she found Jason standing beside the bedroom window, looking outside at the night sky. A crescent moon, surrounded by countless stars, shone down on the dark forest. The wind blowing through the leaves in the treetops was the only sound Mother Nature was making in the forest.

The sun's bright rays shone in through the windows of the bedroom, waking the couple early in the morning. They dressed and walked downstairs to the kitchen. After letting the dogs outside, Jason added fuel to the woodstove. In a brief time, the wood was burning, heating the cooktop on the stove enough to boil water. The couple were soon joined in the kitchen by Joe and Mary. Wendy brewed coffee and the friends sat around the kitchen table discussing their personal lives and their future goals.

Kuzih, hearing the activity downstairs, joined the adults in the kitchen. He climbed on Wendy's lap, snuggling into her chest before falling back asleep. Wendy laid her son on the couch in the living room, wrapping a blanket around her sleeping child. Wendy and Jason left the house shortly thereafter to walk to Samuel's store in Dawson.

Samuel greeted the couple upon their arrival, happy to have their help in getting the place in order. Following Samuel's instructions, soon the items in the store were on display in their rightful places. Sam had ordered extra stock, not wanting to run out of merchandise quickly. He had built a large storage area onto his store, to accommodate the extra inventory. Joe and Mary would be arriving shortly, allowing Samuel to make his first sale. The Grand Re-Opening Sale was beginning tomorrow, and he was expecting a large crowd of eager customers to buy his updated ironware products. Samuel carried items which were hard to find this far north, knowing the market was huge and doing so would someday make him a rich man.

CHAPTER FIVE

Joe and Mary arrived at Samuel's store before lunch. The couple were accompanied by Jason and Wendy's donkey Omar, with Kuzih happily riding on the animal's back. Wendy reached out and removed her son from Omar's back. She secured Omar to the railing out front, which had been built for such a purpose. When they entered the store, Joe and Mary were surprised at the quality of the merchandise Samuel was selling. The store sold other products, such as metal tools, and dog sled items, including harnesses and runners for sleds. If a man had a set of runners, he could usually build the sled on top of them himself.

Mary selected some items for the cabin, while Joe picked up six steel leg traps to replace those he had lost or broken last winter. Joe and Mary had purchased items from Samuel's store last year, including kitchenware and tools. The couple had also replaced their iron fireplace set, which had been original to the cabin. Good quality fireplace tools were important when burning wood was the only heat source. Joe and Mary looked at new woodstoves and stove pipes. Samuel told the couple he would have them delivered to their cabin if they purchased them today.

Joe and Mary's fur trapping season had yielded a bumper crop of fur, which they sold when prices were high, exceeding the amount of money they expected to earn by a third. Joe purchased the stove, telling Samuel to include their other purchases in the delivery. They would not need the services of Omar for moving anything, much to the donkey's delight. Samuel told Joe and Mary he would have the stove delivered in a week.

The entourage left Samuel alone to finish the last minute touches to the store before his opening tomorrow. He had a surprise for the people of Dawson. He had installed a candy counter, not just for the few children living Dawson, but also for the adults with a sweet tooth. He had purchased the candy while staying in Seattle last winter, and it had been included in his merchandise shipment.

Honey, Millie, and Baby Jack, the other donkeys living in Wendy and Jason's barn, were glad to see Omar back, wondering why he had returned without any cargo. Jason inspected the gates of the donkeys' enclosures. He had purchased shiny metal hinges to replace the rusty ones on the doors of the donkeys' pens, planning to do so tomorrow. The group fed and watered the donkeys and chickens in the barn, before returning to the house.

Joe and Mary would spend one more night with Wendy and Jason before heading home to their cabin. Jason and Joe decided to take the canoe out on the lake and hunt waterfowl for dinner. The birds were returning from their migration south and were plentiful on the lake situated on their property. The men launched the canoe and paddled out onto the calm waters. They headed toward the wetland area of the lake, the most probable place to find aquatic birds.

Small flocks of ducks flew overhead, heading in the same direction Jason and Joe were paddling their canoe. Jason and Joe imagined the delicious aroma of duck cooking over the outside fire tonight. A shooting gallery of ducks lay before them; the men drew closer before laying their canoe paddles down, replacing them with their rifles. A succession of shots rang out, leaving four dead birds floating in the water.

The men retrieved the ducks, happily paddling home with dinner. The waterfowl were a treat from Mother Nature. Birds and fish harvested from the lake were an important source of food during the summer, as a lack of refrigeration meant a change of diet during the warm weather months. The ducks the men had shot would be eaten for dinner tonight, a meal everyone in the cabin was looking forward to, especially King and Rusty, the two canine members of the family.

CHAPTER SIX

Jason and Joe beached the canoe along the shoreline and pulled the craft out of the water up onto the grass. Joe retrieved the ducks from the bottom of the canoe, while Jason grabbed their rifles. The men walked to the fur shed, where they left the birds on the worktable. They returned to the house to tell their wives of their success hunting. After a brief rest and a cup of coffee, the men returned to the shed to clean the ducks they would be eating for dinner tonight.

Samuel's Grand Re-Opening Sale was busy; it seemed half of the population of Dawson was in attendance. However, Samuel noticed a significant drop in sales, compared to last year's Grand Opening. Many people had apparently attended just to look, as they had no money to spend on these luxury items. When the gold rush crowds left Dawson, they left a hole in the money supply. This was something Samuel had not taken into account when he decided to open his business.

Sam began to worry sales would be much slower this summer than he anticipated. However, the local fur trappers who worked the forests around Dawson might become new customers. These men were flush with money, as the price of furs had increased due to demand from the European market. Now was a good time for these men to replace some of their tools which had outlived their effectiveness.

Samuel was thinking about supplementing his income this winter by becoming a fur broker. Last year, an Indigenous man, who lived in a village in the bush, had come into his store looking to barter furs for merchandise. This exchange of goods had piqued Samuel's interest in buying furs off the local trappers. He was sure he would be staying in Dawson this winter, as he had another load of product being delivered in mid-September. His brother, Dave, would be travelling with the order, which included additional items for general use around a cabin, six more woodstoves, and extra stove pipes. These latter items were in big demand in town and the surrounding area. His current shipment had included four woodstoves, two of which were already sold. One had been sold to Joe, and the other to the North West Mounted Police to heat an addition which was being built onto the police station.

After the re-opening of Samuel's store, business was slow for two weeks. Then business picked up, as more people living in the area and people passing through Dawson stopped in his store. Axes, saws, iron wedges, and heavy iron hammers were among the first items Sam sold out of. His next delivery of goods would include more of these popular items, but he made a point of remembering to order a larger quantity of these products for next spring. Word spread across the north as to the fine wares Samuel sold, gaining him a reputation as an honest businessman who was always willing to give his customer a fair deal. Samuel was happy, feeling his store was getting off on the right foot, and he had made a wise business decision.

Samuel offered Jason and Wendy part time jobs at his store. He wanted Wendy to work inside, as a clerk, and Jason to deliver woodstoves and pipes, helping with installations if needed. Kuzih would be looked after by one or the other of his parents, while they were individually working for Samuel. He promised to arrange their schedules to allow one of them to be home at all times. The couple agreed to help him with his extended summer hours. During the slow winter months, Samuel would take care of his store himself.

CHAPTER SEVEN

The first rays of sunlight shone through the bedroom window. Jason was meeting Samuel at the store early this morning. Today he was delivering the woodstove and pipes to Joe and Mary's cabin in the forest. Samuel had purchased an ox from Luke, the owner of the livery stable, and a used cart from Phil, the owner of the moving company. He needed the ox and cart to allow him to offer delivery service.

Until Samuel found a more permanent home for his ox, he would be boarded at the livery stable. The man who ran the stable had built a large barn at the back of his property twenty years ago. He used this building to keep larger animals, such as oxen and cows, safely confined. Samuel was to pick up the ox, before meeting Jason at the store. Jason and Samuel had loaded the woodstove and pipes onto the wagon late yesterday, which was now parked outside the store's storage shed. Shortly after Jason's arrival, he hooked the ox to the cart, said goodbye to Samuel, and was on his way to Joe and Mary's cabin.

The ox was in no hurry as he pulled the wagon down the hard packed trail. Three hours later, their presence was announced by a barking Rusty, who alerted Joe and Mary to their company. Jason parked the wagon and he and Joe unloaded the partially assembled stove, stove pipes, and other purchases Joe and Mary had made. The men piled everything together near the cabin door. Joe told Jason he and Mary would be able to handle installing the new stove in the cabin, and invited Jason in for a cool drink and something to eat.

Thirty minutes later, Jason said goodbye to Joe and Mary, driving the ox back toward Dawson. Two hours into their trip, a sudden storm came up, an early season thunderstorm making its appearance. Jason found shelter under the canopy of a large tree. The rain poured down in torrents, soaking the dry dirt on the trail, turning it into slippery mud.

The remainder of the trip to Dawson took longer than usual, as the ox pulled the wagon down the muddy trail. Unfortunately for Jason, by the time they reached Dawson, he was covered in mud from the hooves of the ox, whose every step threw mud on him. When he reached Samuel's store, the store was empty, Samuel having gone home for the day. Jason dropped off the wagon behind the store and returned the ox to the livery stable, placing the animal in the barn out back. Jason then walked home to Wendy.

Taking one look at her husband, Wendy made Jason strip and wash the mud off himself in the lake before allowing him into the house. After doing so, the couple sat around the kitchen table as Jason explained to Wendy how he ended up covered in mud. Wendy laughed at Jason's misfortune, happy he was home.

CHAPTER EIGHT

While Wendy had been waiting for Jason to get home from Joe and Mary's cabin, Samuel had stopped by the house to ask her if she could work at his store for three hours. An important issue had come up which he needed to attend to today. A customer was supposed to be coming into the store to look at a woodstove and he did not want to miss him. Instead of locking up the business, he asked Wendy if she would come in until he returned from his errand.

Wendy obliged Samuel's request, reminding him Kuzih would be accompanying her. Samuel agreed, knowing it was hard for a child to break anything in an ironware store. Once Wendy arrived, Samuel travelled to the office of the local sawmill operator, who had supplied the timbers and cut lumber to build his store. He wanted to purchase enough lumber to build an enclosed barn to house an ox, as well as a shed he could work out of. Samuel wanted to create a space to buy and store fur from Indigenous and local trappers. He was hoping to make a profit from men who were looking to make a quick dollar by selling their furs.

The sawmill owner told Samuel he had time to accompany him to the store now to take measurements, and, if they could agree on a price, he would start preparing his order tomorrow. The owner was certain he had enough wood, stacked and dried, in his lumber yard to fulfill Sam's requirements. The man accompanied Samuel back to his store. Together they looked at the space Sam had on his land and developed a plan for the building's dimensions. They decided to build one large building, half of which could house livestock, while the other half could be used for buying and storing furs.

The sawmill owner took measurements and came up with a rough estimate of the amount of lumber such a build would require. After coming up with a figure for the wood, Samuel was more than happy with the estimated price and told the mill owner to proceed. The man told Samuel he should expect delivery in one week. Shaking hands, the men departed ways and Samuel returned to the inside of his store.

Wendy was happy to see Samuel, as Kuzih was growing restless. She told Sam she had sold one of the two remaining woodstoves to the customer he had been expecting. The buyer left a cash deposit with her and would return to the store within a week to pay the remainder of what he owed for the stove. At that time, he would also arrange for Samuel to deliver the stove to his home.

The customer lived outside of Dawson and had asked if there was anyone who could help him with the stove's installation. Wendy had assured the man her husband would be able to do so, including replacing the stovepipes, which he had also agreed to purchase. This pleased the man greatly, as he felt he could not perform this task safely by himself.

Samuel was pleased Wendy had handled the sale and

there was now only one remaining stove to sell. Woodstoves were the most expensive items Samuel had in his store, and with six more stoves coming on the next shipment of merchandise, he preferred to be sold out of stoves before they arrived. Although, he was certain he would sell all the stoves he had ordered before the cold days of winter set in. Samuel thanked Wendy for her help, sending her and Kuzih home to wait for Jason. He locked up his ironware store, happily walking home to feed his lonely and hungry dog, Spearmint.

CHAPTER NINE

Spearmint met Samuel at the front door. As soon as the door was open, the dog ran past Samuel heading for the nearest tree. Samuel laughed as he watched his dog do his duty against the trunk of the aspen tree. When finished, Spearmint returned to Samuel's side and they entered the house. The day had turned cloudy and dark, so Samuel lit the oil lamps to provide some light and lit a fire in the woodstove to remove the chill from the house.

After playing with Spearmint for a half hour, Samuel served himself and his dog a dinner of smoked venison, which he had bartered for at the store. A trapper had come in looking for an axe, but had no cash. The man did have a large amount of smoked venison, offering to trade Samuel food for an axe. Samuel agreed to the proposition, with both parties happy with the deal.

A sudden ruckus outside the house caught Samuel's attention. He got up from his chair and looked out the window, where he observed flames shooting high up into the sky. A block away, a house was on fire. Sam pulled on his boots and grabbed his jacket, rushing to the scene of the fire. The old wooden house had no chance of withstanding the inferno, burning to the ground almost immediately. The firemen said faulty stovepipes were the cause of the blaze. The owner had been lucky to escape this tragedy unharmed, left to live another day.

Samuel left the scene, realizing how quickly tragedy can strike when living where the unseen forces of nature challenge life everyday. He returned to his cozy home and reunited with his loving pet, Spearmint. Thankful for all that he had, Samuel lay in his bed, fatigue overtaking him. The night had grown quiet, with only the chirping crickets breaking the silence which surrounded Dawson.

Later in the week, Samuel rose early, getting ready for another day at his ironware store. He planned on taking Spearmint with him to work today, knowing he would need to restrain his dog inside the store, afraid Spearmint would run off if left to roam outside on his own. The temptation of exploring new territory would be difficult for the dog to resist. Finding a girlfriend was Spearmint's biggest desire, and he reasoned he would never find love sitting at home. Obviously, Spearmint would not find love sitting in the ironware store either.

Upon entering his store, Samuel noticed the candy counter needed to be replenished. Children and adults alike visited his store for the sole purpose of buying candy. Wendy came to work at noon, relieving Samuel of his duties at the store. She greeted Spearmint, whom she had not seen since last year. Shortly after Samuel left, two loads of lumber arrived for the new building. Two oxen pulled each wagon, loaded with timber. Samuel had driven stakes in the ground earlier, to show where the lumber should be placed. The men unloaded the wagons and Wendy told them Samuel would stop by the sawmill to pay the balance of what he owed. The workers agreed to pass this message along to their boss when they returned to the sawmill.

Wendy worked on some changes Samuel wanted to make to the interior of the store, moving stock around. She was busy with this task when Jason and Kuzih walked into the building. Jason was here to load the wagon with the stove to be delivered to the police station in Dawson. His son helped him carry some of the lighter items from the store, placing them on the wagon. Samuel returned to work, happy to see both of his friends at the store at the same time, friends he depended on more with each passing day.

CHAPTER TEN

J ason arrived at the ironware store early. He let himself into the building using the key Samuel had given him and Wendy before leaving for Seattle last winter. Samuel had told the couple to keep the key, treating Wendy and Jason not only as friends, but also as store employees. Jason was waiting for the livery stable to open to pick up Samuel's ox. He had stopped at the business on his way into town, but the proprietor had not arrived to work yet.

After waiting for thirty minutes, Jason decided to walk the two blocks to the livery stable. He was sure the owner would be there, and he could pick up Samuel's ox to move the stove. Upon arriving at the stable, Luke came out to greet Jason. He had a thriving business in Dawson and an impeccable reputation for how he treated his customers and the animals he cared for. Luke boarded and sold pack animals, with donkeys and mules being the two most popular breeds he dealt with. He had a barn in the back of his property, where he boarded animals, such as oxen, horses, and donkeys.

One of the biggest challenges in running a livery stable was having a steady supply of feed available year round.

Luke experimented with various grains and grasses he could have delivered during the late summer and early fall. He made a special mash for pack animals and had even created a dry dog food, which, if stored properly, remained edible for months. Luke looked after the horses the North West Mounted Police used during the summer months, supplying their food and reshoeing the horses if needed. Luke had two of the Mounties' horses under his watchful eyes, boarded in a special area of his barn, away from the pack animals. The Mounties were responsible for grooming their own horses, this task performed by the constables assigned to the animals.

The Mounted Police utilized the horses to patrol the trails which connected cabins in the forest. The well-being of the men and women living in this wilderness enclave were the responsibility of the North West Mounted Police force. Teaching safety and survival skills to these sometimes inexperienced trappers often meant saving their lives. The Mounties had small cabins built throughout the bush around Dawson. While on patrol, they would use these cabins for shelter, but not while on horseback. The first year the horses were introduced in Dawson, a large grizzly bear attacked and killed one of the prized animals while tethered outside one of the utility cabins in the forest. It was a hard lesson learned by a greenhorn, who had been transferred to Dawson from a district down south.

After a long conversation with Luke, Jason headed to the ironware store with Daisy, Samuel's ox. When the duo reached the store, Samuel was present. He helped Jason hook Daisy to the wagon she was going to pull. The men loaded the heaviest part of the stove, which Jason had been unable to load yesterday when he was alone. Samuel told Jason he had stopped at the Mountie's headquarters yesterday and informed the constable in charge the new stove would be arriving this morning. The man told Samuel they would watch for the delivery, looking forward to getting the stove for their new addition. With that thought in mind, Jason left, leading Daisy to the North West Mounted Police headquarters located a short distance away. He would drop off the stove, but not before having an unexpected adventure on the way.

CHAPTER ELEVEN

Jason walked Daisy toward the police headquarters. The ox displayed but one forward movement, slow and steady. After a fifteen-minute walk, they arrived at their destination. Two constables came out of the building to help Jason unload the wagon. They carried the cast iron appliance and the new stove pipes to the new addition, where it would be installed later. After a brief conversation with the Mounties, Jason left the station, leading Daisy back to the livery stable where Samuel boarded the ox.

Luke met Jason when he arrived at the stable, telling Jason the man sitting inside had been waiting for him to return. He was a dock worker, who was looking for help. A paddle wheeler, piloted by an inexperienced captain, had run aground when it was attempting to dock. Strong currents during the spring can change the structure of the river, causing excess sand to form new sandbars. If a boat captain fails to recognize the signs of such a formation, running aground is a distinct possibility.

The man from the dock introduced himself as Joe. He told Jason the boat was stuck thirty feet from the dock. Joe had come to the livery stable looking for a team of oxen to pull the boat off the sandbar. Luke told Joe, the only ox in town was out on a delivery and was unsure if a single ox would be of much help. Joe said he would wait for the ox to return, hoping his boss's plan of using a rope and pulley would provide enough power to free the boat.

After listening to Joe, Jason patted Daisy on the head and told Joe he would be happy to try to help. Jason and Daisy followed Joe back to the dock, Jason laughing to himself quietly when he saw all the commotion being displayed over the stuck paddle wheeler. Joe went and found his boss, who had sent him to the livery stable to find an animal to help. The men had secured a strong rope to the boat, fed it through a pulley, and were waiting to attach it to Daisy. Once they were ready, Jason edged Daisy forward, the rope tightening as Daisy pulled hard.

The crowd watching from the dock grew quiet, waiting to see what would happen. Jason continued to coax Daisy forward. With one, hard last pull, the riverboat moved, sliding off the sandbar into deeper water. The crowd cheered from the dock and Daisy was considered a hero. Fifteen minutes later, the boat was safely docked, with the captain breathing a sigh of relief. Jason took Samuel's ox back to the livery stable, where she was fed her fill of premium grains, which were purchased by the grateful owner of the stuck paddle wheeler. Daisy had successfully freed the boat from the Yukon River, a formidable foe.

CHAPTER TWELVE

With Daisy safely back in the livery stable and Sam's wagon parked at his store, Jason walked home to his waiting wife and child. He told Wendy about Daisy pulling the paddleboat off the sandbar. Wendy remarked about the ox's strength and how lucky the captain was Daisy was able to free his boat. Wendy and Jason decided to take the canoe and quietly paddle around their lake after lunch. They wanted to observe the abundant wildlife which called this place home.

The day was sunny and warm as the couple launched their canoe into the pristine, blue water of the lake. King, the family dog, barked from the shoreline until the canoe was out of sight. Kuzih enjoyed riding in the canoe. He was an excellent swimmer and loved to be around the water. Wendy and Jason had no fears taking their son in the canoe with them, even though the waters could be unpredictable at times.

The lake was full of birds, with ducks being the dominate waterfowl calling this water home. Kuzih, sitting in the front of the canoe, suddenly became excited and was pointing. Jason and Wendy glanced at what Kuzih was looking at.

A short distance from the canoe was a pair of loons, birds known for their mysterious ways and soulful song. On the mother's back, rode their baby; a convenient way to keep track of where her youngster was on this dangerous water.

Kuzih kept pointing at the abundant wildlife which called this ecosystem home. He spotted a deer drinking water from the shoreline, a blue heron standing like a statue, waiting for his dinner to swim by, and a soaring eagle circling high above them. These were but a few of the occupants living in this pristine environment in Canada's north.

Wendy and Jason paddled quietly across the calm water. The canoe moved forward; the couple mesmerized by the beauty of their surroundings. After a pleasant two hours of canoeing, Wendy and Jason returned to their cabin and a surprise. Sitting on the shoreline, waiting for their return, were Wendy's brother, Steward, and his wife, Blossom. Wendy, Jason, and Kuzih exited the canoe and hugged their company. A surprise visit by this couple was always welcomed by Jason and Wendy.

Steward helped Jason pull the canoe from the water and place it under the cover of the evergreen trees which grew nearby. The two couples walked to the house for a visit. Steward and Blossom planned to spend the night, wanting to buy coffee, sugar, and a supply of jerky while in Dawson. Blossom also wanted to visit the ironware store to look at the newest products Samuel was offering for sale. Steward's friend, Tim, who owned a sawmill near Steward and Blossom's home was caring for their dogs while they were gone. This gesture allowed the couple to escape from their daily routine at home, a welcome break from their life in the forest.

CHAPTER THIRTEEN

Food was scarce in the Yukon during the months with no refrigeration. Any wild game or fish harvested needed to be cooked or smoked within six hours of procuring the meat. Steward had shot two rabbits on the trail to Wendy and Jason's house this morning. Jason had stopped on his way home from town and purchased trout from the Indigenous couple who sold fresh fish. Steward suggested they enjoy a dinner outdoors this evening, cooking the rabbit and fish over the open flame of the campfire.

Steward went to Jason's shed to clean the rabbit. The trout Jason had purchased were already gutted and ready to be cooked over the campfire. The setting sun caused twilight to sweep across this wilderness land. When Steward came from the shed with the two cleaned rabbits, the fire Jason had started was burning hot. The men started cooking the rabbit and fish while their wives were inside the house cooking greens and edible roots they had collected from the forest.

The night was clear, with a full moon and a million shining stars illuminating the dark sky. A hungry fox waited in the shadows, hoping to find some food left behind after these family members finished their dinner and retired into the house for the evening. Steward told Wendy he had been helping his friend, Tim, at the sawmill. He had asked Steward to help on a part-time basis, as labor was difficult to find in the remote area where they lived. The demand for lumber had increased, as more people settled in the area, leaving Tim constantly looking for help.

The night air was crisp, the forest quiet. The lonely call of a loon was the only sound to pierce the silence of the night. The couples enjoyed dinner together, after which Jason let the coals of the fire burn down to the embers. The two couples went to bed in the comfort of Jason and Wendy's house, leaving the fox nothing to find, but the bones left from the rabbits eaten for dinner.

The steady sound of hard rain on the roof woke Wendy and Jason from their restful sleep. Lightning lit up the night sky, while thunder shook the windows of the house. Shortly after the couples had retired to bed, this thunderstorm had moved into the area. Wendy had recently planted some of her vegetable garden, making the falling rain a welcome sound. The couple lay in bed listening to the departing storm, as the lightning grew less intense, and the thunder became distant. Fresh cool air flowed through the open bedroom windows, allowing Wendy and Jason to fall back asleep until the morning light woke them to face another day.

CHAPTER FOURTEEN

Steward and Blossom lay in bed listening to the morning bird song, the symphony of music coming in through the open bedroom window. The couple could hear Wendy downstairs working in the kitchen. The odor of fresh brewed coffee found its way upstairs. Steward and Blossom pulled themselves out of bed and followed the smell of the coffee to the kitchen. Wendy greeted the couple with a hug, telling Steward and Blossom Jason had taken the family dogs outside with him. He planned on feeding his sled dogs and the animals in the barn before returning to the house for breakfast.

Wendy told Steward and Blossom they were going to eat eggs this morning, collected from her chickens in the barn. Finished with his chores outside, Jason returned to his house with the eggs, joining his family in the kitchen for breakfast. Steward said he and Blossom wanted to walk into Dawson today to buy a few items, such as coffee, sugar, salt, and jerky. While in town, they planned on visiting the ironware store. Steward wanted to see where his sister and brother-in-law were working and meet Samuel.

The calendar had changed to the month of June.

The wildflowers were blooming in the meadows and the mammals in the forest were busy caring for their young, who were born during the spring. After finishing breakfast, Steward and Blossom excused themselves from the table. The couple left the house, saying goodbye to Wendy and Jason. They walked to the general store in Dawson, where they purchased the commodities they liked to have on hand for everyday use. This was the mercantile they visited often, as the proprietor was welcoming to all Indigenous people, something that was not true of other businesses in town. There had been a recent shift among new arrivals and their attitude toward the native populace, which Steward and many of his family members had noted. After conversing with the friendly owner of the store for a short time, they left to walk to the ironware store, the most popular new business in Dawson.

Upon entering the store, the couple were greeted by Samuel, the owner. Steward introduced himself as Wendy's brother, and Blossom as her sister-in-law. Samuel was very pleased to meet them, as he considered both Wendy and Jason his friends. He said Wendy had talked a lot about her brother and his wife, who lived as fur trappers in the remote forest of the Yukon. Samuel offered Steward and Blossom a ten percent discount on any purchase they made from the store.

After looking at the merchandise, and knowing they could not carry anything big or heavy back to their cabin, the couple purchased some tinware. Samuel carried a line of such products in his store, with cups, plates, and soup bowls being popular selections for customers. Blossom selected these items to upgrade the older utensils they currently used in their kitchen.

When Steward was paying his bill, Samuel reached into the candy counter, removing a variety of hard candies and handing them to Blossom as a welcome gift for visiting his store. The couple and Sam exchanged pleasantries before leaving the store to walk back to Wendy and Jason's house. The couple planned on spending one more night in Dawson before leaving on the two day walk back to their cabin, a place Steward and Blossom would forever long to be.

CHAPTER FIFTEEN

Steward and Blossom left Samuel's store to walk back to Wendy and Jason's house. The sound of barking dogs filled the air as the couple walked past the homes of the people of Dawson. Sled dogs, not used during the summer months, were confined to their chains until the snow made an appearance again. Unsettled and angry, the dogs lunged at the end of their restraints at anyone passing by their yard.

After a short time, the couple walked out of Dawson, arriving at Wendy and Jason's home. King, the family dog, ran to greet the family members he loved dearly. After entering Wendy's yard, the couple continued walking to the front door, with the canine following closely behind them. Entering the house, Steward and Blossom smelled the aroma of something good. Unsure of what they were smelling, Blossom asked Wendy what she was cooking. Wendy laughed, telling Blossom it was a chicken Jason had slaughtered from their chicken coop.

A new brood of chickens, hatched from their eggs, would guarantee the survival of the flock, while some of the mature chickens were culled and used for food during the summer months. While Steward and Blossom were running errands in Dawson, Jason had picked a plump adult chicken to butcher. After grabbing the bird by the neck, much to the displeasure of the other chickens, the struggling bird was taken out to the chopping block. Jason laid the hapless chicken's neck across the face of the wooden block, raised his hatchet, and with one downward swing, the severed head fell onto the ground. Jason released the bird from his grip. The headless chicken danced around the yard until its heart stopped beating. The bird's death was quick, as it fell to the ground never to move again.

Jason retrieved the dead chicken and cleaned the bird. After he finished, he gave the chicken to Wendy to cook for dinner. She was roasting the bird in the oven of the woodstove, with root vegetables she had purchased in Dawson earlier in the week. Blossom offered to help Wendy get dinner ready, but instead, Wendy asked if she and Steward would feed the donkeys in the barn.

When the barn door opened, the donkeys sounded out a welcome greeting in unison, to whomever was entering their domain. The donkeys were always glad when they had human company close by. The presence of people in the barn meant food and affection, two things the donkeys were always looking for.

Steward and Blossom especially liked the youngest donkey, Baby Jack. The couple took him from the barn to a nearby meadow to graze. The growing animal needed good food to remain strong and heathy. Unfortunately for the donkeys, predators lurked everywhere, meaning the animals could not be left alone outside the confines of the safety of their barn. The couple lay in the grassy meadow, letting the warm sunshine relax their tired bodies. Baby Jack was happily eating, picking and choosing his favorite grasses to eat.

After staying in the meadow for an hour, Steward and Blossom returned Baby Jack to the barn. They left shortly afterwards, locking the barn door behind them. They returned to the house to find Samuel had arrived for a visit and was waiting to talk with them.

CHAPTER SIXTEEN

S amuel had run into problems hiring the construction crew he had used last year to build his store. They were busy on another job, which was scheduled to last for several months. This left Samuel with no contractor to help him build the shed and barn for the small fur brokerage business he planned on opening this winter.

The owner of the sawmill, who had supplied the lumber to Samuel, had put him in contact with a contractor in Whitehorse. This gentleman had said he could send an experienced crew of four men to Dawson, but he wanted to be paid half of his fee in cash before sending them to town. Samuel needed someone to take the cash to the contractor and was hoping Steward would be interested in doing this for him.

Steward told Samuel he had too many obligations with his dogs to leave his cabin for any length of time, and suggested Samuel could hire men from his tribe, many of whom were excellent craftsmen. He assured Samuel these men would do a fine job building his new shed. Samuel thought if Steward could put together a local work crew, it would save him a lot of worry. He asked Steward to pursue assembling the builders, agreeing to pay him for his trouble.

Samuel left shaking Steward's hand, hoping their arrangement would work out. He walked back to his store, where two men, with an ox and wagon, were waiting for him. They told Samuel they were there to buy a woodstove. Samuel told the men they were in luck, as he had only one of these items left to sell. The sun was hot, making the men sweat as they loaded the stove and the accompanying pipes onto their wagon. After paying for the stove, the men left the ironware store, the ox lumbering down the dusty streets of Dawson.

Two hours went by, without a single customer coming into the store. Samuel decided to close his business early and walk home. Soon after locking up the building, he opened his front door, only to be greeted by Spearmint, who lavished him with kisses. Samuel decided to take his dog for a walk to the river, interested in seeing if there were any riverboats in town.

Arriving at the docks, a flurry of activity was going on. A riverboat had just arrived in Dawson, loaded with goods from Whitehorse. Boxes of canned goods, including coffee and sugar, were being unloaded, heading to the two general stores in town. Supplies for the feed store were being picked up by the owner, as Samuel watched. Two mules pulling a cart was the mode of transportation to get the bags of feed back to his stables.

As Sam watched the activity unfolding in front of him, he rubbed Spearmint's head, wondering if following this dream had been the right decision. Samuel was thinking opening his store may have been a poor choice. He had not accounted for the logistics of getting the products from the foundry to Dawson, nor factored in the expense involved in shipping the items. Samuel was losing money, unforeseen when he started this venture.

Samuel came to a decision. After the second barge of wares arrived in mid-September, he would restock the store with the new merchandise. He would finish building the shed he had purchased the lumber for and spend the winter in Dawson running his business. He hoped to buy and sell furs from the shed he was building, a new venture for him.

However, when most of his inventory was sold, he would close the store and the fur brokerage, selling the buildings to recoup some of his losses in his failed business attempts. This was a secret he would tell no one, including Wendy and Jason. For now, Samuel would continue his life, with business as usual.

CHAPTER SEVENTEEN

An early morning breeze blew through the bedroom window. Jason opened his eyes, his nose catching the aroma of coffee, drifting up from the kitchen. Wendy had awakened earlier and was preparing her husband breakfast. Today he was going to deliver and install the woodstove she had sold when Samuel was out of the store. The purchaser's name was Jordan and he lived outside of Dawson. Jason figured it would take at least an hour to get to his house using the ox and wagon. The woodstove would need to be carried one hundred yards off the main trail, to the trapper's home deep in the bush. Jordan also had arranged for Jason to help with the installation of the new stove and pipes, as well as the removal of his old woodstove.

At breakfast, Jason told Wendy he expected to be gone most of the day. Hugging and kissing his wife and his son goodbye, Jason left the house for Samuel's store. The sun was shining, and the day was warm. After reaching Dawson, Jason stopped at the livery stable to pick up Daisy, Samuel's ox. She would be pulling the wagon with the stove and pipes Jason was delivering today. Daisy was always a cooperative animal, willing to go anywhere she was asked. Jason and

Daisy worked well together, sharing a mutual respect and fondness for each other, which were unwavering.

Jason led Daisy to Samuel's store and hooked her to the wagon. Samuel had arrived to work early and loaded the woodstove on the wagon. He had secured the items for the bumpy ride down the rut-filled trail to the trapper's isolated cabin. Jason said goodbye to Samuel, as he led Daisy toward their destination. After a thirty-minute walk, the forest grew denser, making the trail more difficult to maneuver. It proved to be challenging to keep the ox and cart from getting caught in the thick underbrush which lined the path.

After a grueling ninety minutes of travel, Jason reached the footpath which led to the man's cabin. The trapper had left a red cloth tied to a tree limb to mark the way. Jason unhooked Daisy from the wagon, not wanting to leave the ox alone in the forest. Predators were always lurking nearby, hunting for something to eat. Jason decided to tie the ox beside the cabin while the men worked on removing the old stove and installing the new one.

A short distance from the trail, Jason approached the trapper's cabin. He yelled out to Jordan, who stepped out of his cabin with his dog at his side. The man shook hands with Jason, telling him they would work together on the removal and installation of the new woodstove. First, the men disconnected the old stove pipes and carried them outside. They removed the woodstove from the cabin, placing it behind the shed.

After this job was completed, the two men made many trips from the wagon, carrying stove parts. Working over the course of five hours, the job was finally finished with the new stove in place. The trapper lit a fire in his new woodstove, happy with the results. Jordan was relieved to have a safe environment; his old stove and pipes no longer posing a danger. He realized the outdated pipes could have easily caught fire and burned his cabin down. Thanking Jason for his help, the two men shook hands.

Jason gathered up Daisy and led the animal back to the wagon. The walk back to Dawson was easier, as the wagon was empty. The duo reached the store without mishap. Samuel had left for the day, but Jason positioned the wagon behind the store before unhooking Daisy. He then led the ox back to the livery stable, feeding and watering her before going home to his waiting wife and child.

CHAPTER EIGHTEEN

W hen Jason arrived home, he was surprised to see Steward, his wife's brother, at his house. Steward had come to Dawson to see Samuel about the construction of his new building. He had found four men who were willing to come to Dawson to work. He had scheduled the men's arrival for a week from now, the Indigenous workers planning to camp on Samuel's property until the construction of the building was completed. Steward had stopped in at the ironware store while Jason was making the delivery. Samuel was pleased with the arrangements Steward had made and paid him for his assistance.

Steward planned on spending the night with Wendy and Jason, before starting his walk home in the morning. Blossom had stayed at the couple's cabin to care for their huskies, which included a new litter of puppies. Wendy had prepared a scrumptious meal of bear meat for her brother and husband. The Mounties had shot a troublesome bear, who had been marauding the streets of Dawson at night looking for food. They had dropped off some of the meat to be distributed to those in need with Wendy this morning, allowing her to take one roast for herself. Potatoes and fresh baked bread rounded out the dinner menu, which the siblings and Jason ate together.

After dinner, Jason and Steward retired to the living room to socialize while Wendy cleaned up the kitchen and washed the dishes. The men talked about Samuel's venture into the fur brokerage business. Steward suggested to Jason if his business fared well, the trappers living in the forest would sell their furs to him in the spring. Wendy soon joined them in the living room, bringing each man a small bowl of berries she had picked earlier in the day.

The month of June was almost over, leaving the Yukon on the cusp of summer. Campfires would soon burn more than woodstoves, as the ambience of being able to enjoy the outside environment became a priority for these isolated men and women. In this harsh land of forests and wilderness lakes, residents were entombed in their cabins for months on end, only going outdoors to complete needed tasks. They are unable to enjoy nature due to the bitter cold which grips Canada's north during the winter.

Steward turned in early, as he wanted to leave at daybreak. Before heading upstairs, he told Jason and Wendy he would say his goodbyes now, so they did not have to get up with him. As he lay down on the comfortable bed, with a goose down pillow under his head, a light breeze blew in through the open window. A howl from a lone wolf broke the silence which enveloped the dark night. The leaves rustling in the wind lulled Steward to sleep, until the first rays of light streamed in through the window, waking him to start another day. Steward rose from the bed, quietly leaving the house before anyone else was stirring. Closing the front door behind him, he carried only his rifle and a knapsack for his two-day walk home, a destination which meant a reunion with his wife, whom Steward hated to leave alone.

CHAPTER NINETEEN

L eaving Wendy and Jason's home at daybreak, with only a small amount of jerky to eat on the way, Steward carried a rifle slung across his shoulder. He was a seasoned hunter, having spent years living alone in the forests of Canada's Yukon. After meeting Blossom, the couple settled into a wilderness cabin and a more sedentary lifestyle in the bush. Steward loved sled dogs, raising and selling huskies from his home. Steward's dogs had a reputation for being strong, healthy animals. He treated his sled dogs well, keeping them fed, watered, and loved. The animals' shelters were kept clean, at times a formidable task for Steward and Blossom to perform.

The sun shone down brightly on Steward as he made his journey through the forest. Steward shot a rabbit he encountered on the trail, the animal enjoying the sunshine and paying no heed to the danger around him. The rabbit's lack of sensibilities meant dinner for Steward tonight. The late afternoon brought Steward to the lake, which was the halfway point of his journey home. He set up camp for the evening, gathering firewood to cook the rabbit. Twilight settled over the beautiful lake, as Steward sat on the shore, his campsite overlooking the pristine water. Ducks and geese were active, flying over the lake, looking for a safe place to spend the night.

Lighting his campfire, wisps of smoke rose skyward before the kindling took to flame. Soon a robust fire was burning, as Steward cleaned the rabbit he had shot earlier. Using a sharpened stick for a cooking utensil, he placed the rabbit over the fire. The light from the full moon and the shining stars showed the true beauty of the wilderness surrounding the campsite. The lonely call of the loon filled the night with sound. The crackling fireplace and the aroma of the rabbit cooking caught the attention of a hungry fox. The animal waited in the shadows, hoping for a taste of what Steward was cooking.

Steward lay on his back, wishing on a star. His thoughts were of Blossom, his wife whom he longed to see. Steward fell asleep on the hard ground, the coals in the firepit burning down to embers, sending its last gasp of smoke drifting into the forest. Steward slept peacefully, as silence crept into the darkness of the night. Dawn would soon arrive, indicating the start of another day. Steward's journey would end, reuniting him with his wife, Blossom, in their cabin in the woods, a place the couple called home.

CHAPTER TWENTY

Samuel left his house early with his dog Spearmint, having arranged to meet a customer at his store early this morning. The man was to retrieve items he had purchased yesterday but could not transport until today. Shortly after Sam's arrival, the customer showed up with a mule pulling a cart. After pleasantries were exchanged, Samuel helped the man load his items into the cart. The customer told Sam he was taking the purchases to a friend who had recently built a cabin outside of town. This friend owned a dog team but had no way to move goods during the summer. The new homeowner was trying to prepare before the snow and cold of winter arrived, relying on his friend to help.

Samuel stood in the doorway of the store, waving goodbye to the man as the mule pulled the cart away from the store. When he turned around to re-enter the building, he looked around at the interior and realized he had sold half of the goods which arrived by barge earlier in the year. His brother David was arriving with another load of ironware in mid-September. This would be the last order of ironware Samuel would place, as in the spring he would try to sell the building and move back to Seattle. He knew he made a mistake when he embraced the north and realized the north would never embrace him back.

The Indigenous men Samuel was expecting to come and build his new building would be arriving today. The leader of the work crew had stopped by the store earlier in the week to look at the job site. Samuel had liked the man, who had returned to tell his men what they needed to carry to the work site in Dawson. He believed Steward had selected a good group of tradesmen to erect the barn and fur shed.

As the day wore on, business was slow, causing Samuel to close his store. He decided to take Spearmint to play with King, while he visited with Wendy and Jason at their home. As Samuel and his dog walked through the quiet streets of Dawson toward the outskirts of the city, he felt the tranquillity which surrounded him. It was a feeling only nature could provide in this untamed land.

Samuel soon found himself knocking at Jason's front door. Surprised to see him, Jason invited his friend in for coffee and hot rolls. Samuel never refused the hospitality Wendy and Jason offered. King and Spearmint stayed outdoors to enjoy each other's company. Samuel entered the house and took a seat in the kitchen, where he relished a cup of coffee and a hot roll, fresh from the oven.

Samuel told the couple he was expecting the work crew Steward had arranged to construct his new building to arrive today. He was hopeful the project would only take a week, as the building was not large and most of the lumber had been cut to size at the sawmill. When Sam was leaving, Wendy remarked to Samuel she and her family might come by the store to see her cousin, who was part of the work crew.

Upon arriving at his store, Samuel saw two horses, their backs piled high with goods the construction crew had brought with them. Within two hours, the men had their camp set up, complete with a campfire for cooking. The men had brought fresh venison for dinner, planning to entertain and get to know their new employer tonight. The workers had also carried smoked fish, smoked duck, and moose jerky, which they had prepared at their village for this work assignment in town.

Jason, Wendy, and their son, Kuzih, arrived at the store in the latter part of the afternoon. A small crowd had gathered to watch the strangers erect their camp, which was causing excitement in the town of Dawson. Although many residents had lived side by side with Indigenous neighbors and accepted them as friends, there had recently been an undercurrent of bigotry among Dawson's newer citizens. Some of the crowd were merely intrigued by the workers as they watched them get settled, while others were alarmed by seeing the men preparing for what could be an extended stay. Wendy found her cousin among a group of onlookers who had entered the store to buy candy from Samuel's candy counter. He shared some of his treats with Kuzih, who had a sweet tooth of his own. Wendy was glad to meet the other members of the building crew and invited them to come for a visit some evening, if they had the time.

As luck would have it, a few of the townspeople in the crowd had entered the store and found things they could not do without. Over the next few days, Samuel's sales increased, until the crowd became bored with watching the construction and moved on. The work crew displayed a high degree of professionalism and completed the building in the expected time. Samuel was pleased with the arrangement he had made with Steward, paying the work crew a little more than the agreed upon price.

The following morning, the men packed up their belongings and left for home before Samuel arrived at the store. He was expecting Jason to stop by the store early, to help add some of the finishing touches to his new building. Luke, from the livery stable, was also expected, as he was going to deliver a load of bedding for Daisy's new home and enough food to keep her fed until the fall. Luke had told Samuel he was waiting for his last load of supplies to arrive via the Yukon River from Whitehorse. He needed to restock his livery stable before winter, as the people of Dawson expected him to have food for their hungry animals if they needed it.

Jason's arrival coincided with Luke's, and they worked together to unload the straw from Luke's wagon to Daisy's new pen in the barn. Jason accompanied Luke back to the stables to retrieve Daisy and lead her to her new home at Samuel's business. A new life for Daisy was about to begin, a life the ox was sure to enjoy.

CHAPTER
TWENTY-ONE

J ason walked Daisy to her new barn, making sure the animal was comfortable before he left for home. Returning home to his waiting wife and son, the trio enjoyed hot rolls from the oven, smothered in Wendy's homemade jam for lunch, as they discussed their plans for the afternoon. Since it was a lovely day, the couple decided to take the canoe out onto the lake. Wendy and Jason knew Kuzih would enjoy the fresh air and the beauty of nature which surrounded them when they were on the water.

The trio walked to the lake and retrieved the canoe from its resting place under the evergreen trees. Jason picked up the craft and placed it in the water. Kuzih wanted to be the navigator, sitting in the front of the canoe. Wendy agreed, taking her position in the middle section of the boat, with Jason sitting in the back. Jason controlled the canoe's direction with his paddle, while Wendy shared the paddling duties with her husband.

The mid-July day was warm, the hot sun shining down on the canoers as the craft slid gracefully across the calm water of the lake. Kuzih pointed skyward at the ducks and other waterfowl flying near the canoe. He spotted a moose feeding in marshland along the shoreline, the animal's majestic shoulders and rack of antlers a testament to his authority in the forest. Wendy and Jason paddled the canoe back to their house, with their son asleep in the bow. The hour the trio spent on the water was enough, as all three of them were sunburned and needed to get out of the sun and into the shade.

When the canoe hit the shoreline, Kuzih woke up. He climbed out of the canoe onto the shore, waiting for his parents to disembark. Once his dad placed the canoe in its rightful place under the evergreen trees, the group walked home to escape the scathing rays of the sun. Thunder from a storm in the distance could be heard. Twenty minutes later, a cooling rain fell from the sky as the thunder boomed nearby. Steam rose from the hot earth; nature's power on display as the land was doused with refreshing water, ending the discomfort the excessive heat had caused.

Jason, Wendy, their son, and the family dog, King, spent the remainder of the day inside. The storm had cooled the air and left a breeze blowing through the open windows of the house. Wendy and Jason felt at this moment there was no other place they would rather be. The Yukon would always be their home.

CHAPTER
TWENTY-TWO

The lazy days of summer in the Dawson area would soon be coming to an end. The calendar had turned to August two weeks ago and the first hint of the change of seasons was in the air. Samuel had sold most of the merchandise he had in his ironware store, only the most unpopular items were still available. Samuel was waiting for his brother, Dave, to arrive in Dawson, along with the goods he had ordered for the winter. He was expected the second week of September, arriving from Whitehorse on a paddle wheeler pushing the barge loaded with merchandise for the store. It was a treacherous journey, four hundred miles down the mighty Yukon River. The order included six woodstoves, axes, saws, snowshoes, dogsled supplies, and runners. Samuel had also requisitioned extra sets of stove pipes, always an item in big demand. Metal tripods, for use over campfires or in fireplaces, were a new product Samuel would sell in his store this fall.

Daisy had adapted well to her new home in Samuel's barn. Wendy and Jason paid attention to Daisy, visiting regularly to feed the animal and spoil her with treats. Wendy had invited Samuel for dinner at their house, Jason telling him to bring Spearmint with him. King and Spearmint could play together, while Samuel ate dinner with Wendy and Jason. Sam was looking forward to a delicious meal, and he wanted to talk with Jason about building shelves and a workbench for the new fur brokerage business he was opening.

Samuel stayed at his store until 5 p.m., waiting for a customer who owed him money. The man had left with merchandise yesterday, with a promise to pay for his purchase today. Sam was disappointed when the customer was a no show but decided to lock up the store and leave with Spearmint for Wendy and Jason's house. He hoped to see the man tomorrow to collect the money that was owed to him.

A short walk took Samuel and Spearmint to Jason and Wendy's. His knock on the front door attracted King's attention first. King knew his friend, Spearmint, was on the other side, the dog's scent familiar to him. Wendy greeted Samuel, inviting him into the house. He joined Wendy and Jason in the kitchen, sitting at the table. Dinner tonight consisted of beef stew. Beef was a luxury item in Dawson, which Jason had purchased in town. Wendy cooked the meat with a harvest of vegetables from her garden, a rare treat for Samuel.

Over dinner, the men discussed the finish work which needed to be done in Sam's new shed. Jason told Samuel he would be happy to do the work for him. Samuel asked Wendy if she could make a large sign to identify his fur brokerage business. He had already purchased a few furs from trappers, which he was storing in the shed. It was important to Samuel to open his fur buying business as soon as possible, wanting to let the local trappers know his new venture was up and running.

CHAPTER
TWENTY-THREE

After a lengthy conversation with his hosts, Samuel called his dog Spearmint and prepared to leave Wendy and Jason's house. As he left, Jason told Sam he would come to the ironware store early tomorrow to work on building the shelves and workbench in the new shed. The sun was setting as Samuel and his dog began their walk home. Twilight swept over Dawson, giving the town an unnatural light.

When Samuel passed by the livery stable, he noticed Luke was still there, so he stopped for a visit. Luke was a busy man, owning the only stables in town, but he did enjoy chatting with friends, which is how Samuel came to learn about his time in Dawson. Luke's workdays were long during the gold rush era in Dawson, but now things had calmed, as most of the gold seekers and men of adventure had left town. Luke had moved to Dawson from Edmonton seven years ago, after his father died. He had taken care of his sick father, slowly watching him waste away as illness ravished his body. Devasted by his father's death, and enriched by selling his father's property, Luke decided to move to the growing town of Dawson and buy the livery business.

A friend of Luke's had just returned to Edmonton from Dawson and knew the owner of the livery business had suffered an accident and was no longer able to perform the physical labor required to keep the stables open. Luke seized this opportunity, packed his bags and travelled to Dawson. He purchased the livery stable, worked hard, and made the business a success. When gold was discovered in the area, he hired a young man, weak in mind, to help him around the stables. Under Luke's protective umbrella, the man flourished and continued as a trusted employee, working there for the past five years.

Samuel purchased a bag of wild apples from Luke before leaving the stable. He would stop by his store and feed Daisy her favorite treat, apples, before heading home. Daisy was a social animal and did not like being left alone in the new barn. At night she was lonely and afraid, as she sensed predators outside her stall at night, trying to find a way inside. Wendy and Jason had previously offered to move Daisy to their barn. Their building was larger and had donkeys and chickens there to keep Daisy company.

As Samuel fed Daisy her apples, he felt sorry for his lonely animal and decided to take Wendy and Jason up on their offer to keep his ox in the larger and more secure building. Securing the barn, he said goodbye to Daisy and headed home. Once there, he gave Spearmint a moose bone to chew on, while he started a fire in the woodstove. Soon the house was a bastion of comfort, with Samuel sitting in his favorite chair, with his dog snoring by the woodstove. Times like this made Samuel want to stay in Dawson, but life this far north was difficult. Life in Seattle was easier, and more suited to Samuel's lifestyle. His decision to sell his building and land in the spring and leave Dawson was final; his life would continue, just not in the Yukon.

CHAPTER
TWENTY-FOUR

Jason rolled over in the bed, reaching for Wendy sleeping beside him. He pulled her close, snuggling into her back. A cool breeze blew in through the open bedroom window. Jason pulled himself out of bed and retrieved a blanket from the cupboard. He returned to bed, covering Wendy and himself with the heavier covering. The couple snuggled together under the warm blanket Wendy's mother had made for her many years ago. This moment of paradise was interrupted by King. He had heard someone moving around upstairs, which prompted him to bark to let whoever was up know he wanted to be let outside. Jason grudgingly got out of bed, heading downstairs to fulfill his dog's wishes.

While downstairs, Jason added wood to the dying embers in the woodstove and placed a kettle of water on the cooktop to boil. Jason then went back upstairs to get dressed for the day. He passed Wendy on the stairway, who was on her way to the kitchen to bake rolls for breakfast.

Today, Jason was going to begin installing the shelves and workbench in Samuel's recently built shed. Wendy had finished making the sign for the front of the building where

Samuel was housing his fur brokerage business. Jason would take the sign with him and install it before beginning work on the interior.

After eating some freshly baked rolls and jam for breakfast, Jason said goodbye to his wife and son and left the house, kissing them goodbye. He walked into Dawson and soon found himself at the ironware store. Jason went to the back of the store to retrieve a hammer and nails and installed the sign over the door of the shed. Shortly after finishing that job, Samuel arrived with his dog, Spearmint. He told Jason he planned to leave Spearmint in the ironware store, while he assisted Jason in the shed. If a customer came into the store, Spearmint would bark and let him know.

The men got to work, the sounds of the sawing of wood and hammering lasting well into the afternoon. Daisy was entertained watching Jason and Samuel work from behind the partition which separated the ox from the rest of the building. Samuel talked to Jason about moving Daisy to the barn at his house, promising Jason he would pay all expenses related to his ox. Jason told Samuel he and Wendy had already discussed the move, deciding it would be better for Daisy, especially with winter around the corner. The lonely ox would have the donkeys and chickens for company, as well as Kuzih and themselves, who would be there to spoil the large animal.

Jason and Samuel finished their work in the shed, just as the sun was setting. Jason told Samuel goodbye and left for home, anxious to get back to Wendy and Kuzih. Another day had passed, the setting sun reflecting a paradise which could never be copied in this gateway to the north, a land called the Yukon.

CHAPTER
TWENTY-FIVE

After arriving home to his wife and child, Jason ate the dinner Wendy had prepared for him. Not knowing when he would be home from work, she had fed herself and Kuzih an hour earlier. Jason told Wendy about the conversation he and Samuel had regarding Daisy. Wendy agreed to Sam's proposition, suggesting tomorrow they could take Kuzih to retrieve Daisy and bring the ox to her new home.

The night was dark, the cloud-filled sky blocking the light from the stars from reaching the ground. The chirping of crickets was the only sound breaking the silence of the forest which surrounded them. King lay awake, resting by the woodstove. Suddenly the dog lifted his head and listened. The distant howl of a wolf pack signalled a kill, and the call to dinner for the other wolves who had been separated from the pack. Wendy and Jason listened to the wolves howling, their song drifting in through the open bedroom windows. They lay in bed talking about when they lived and trapped in a cabin in the forest. It was a life they chose to leave behind a few years ago, after the death of their beloved aunt.

A pattering of rain on the roof, woke the couple from their peaceful sleep, as the first light of day was streaming in through the bedroom windows. The rain ceased falling shortly thereafter, but left a misty fog throughout the forest. The couple pulled themselves out of bed and dressed for the day. Jason walked downstairs to the kitchen, lit the woodstove, and let King outside. He was soon followed by Wendy and Kuzih. The group ate a quick breakfast of jerky, before leaving their house to move Daisy to her new home in the barn.

On the walk to Samuel's store, the trio happened upon a stray dog. Malnourished and sick, he appeared out of the forest; his survival tested after the sudden death of his owner. The dog, which Kuzih named Rafter, followed them to Samuel's store. Rafter was hoping Wendy and Jason would have pity on him and feed him. Upon reaching the store, Jason did just that, entering the store and retrieving some of Spearmint's dry dog food. The starving dog ate greedily, now thinking Wendy and Jason were his friends.

Much to Kuzih's delight, his parents took Daisy from her place behind the ironware store and led her toward their house, where she would live in the barn with the donkeys and chickens. Their building would make a safer and more comfortable home than where Daisy had been living, behind Samuel's store.

Entering the barn, the entourage was greeted by a chorus of sound. The donkeys welcomed the new resident, and even the chickens were delighted Daisy was moving into the barn. Jason and Wendy got Daisy settled into her new stall and proceeded to feed and water all their animals. They left the barn, leaving the occupants alone to get to know each other better. With Kuzih in hand, the couple returned to the house, pleased Daisy was now in their barn and not alone behind Samuel's store. Daisy could not have been happier with her new living arrangements.

CHAPTER TWENTY-SIX

Rafter had followed Wendy and Jason home, leaving the couple no choice but to keep the dog and nurse him back to health. Rafter was hungry and alone, and needed to be adopted by a responsible owner who would take care of him. Wendy and Jason decided to keep the orphaned husky temporarily, hoping to find him a permanent home. The dog would live outside near the barn, in a shelter Jason would build for him. Rafter would be kept free of chains, allowed to roam Jason and Wendy's property. King did not care about Rafter's presence, if he was outside. The family pet had no intention of sharing his home with this newcomer.

The month of August was coming to an end. A subtle change was taking place, as the first hint of fall made its appearance in the Yukon. The days were getting shorter, while the nights were growing colder. The paddle wheelers and steamboats plying the Yukon River would soon be making their last deliveries of goods to Dawson for the season. Samuel's load of merchandise would be arriving in two weeks from Skagway, via Whitehorse, accompanied by his brother Dave. Samuel had not seen his sibling since early spring and was looking forward to his visit. Dave's assistance in unloading the merchandise from the wagons carrying it from the docks and setting up the displays in the store would be a big help. Dave was planning to spend September in Dawson, before returning to Seattle where he lived.

Jason suggested to Wendy they take Kuzih for a walk to the Dawson riverfront. It was a beautiful day, and the group could watch the increased boat activity along the river. Once the river froze up, it would be impossible for riverboats to use the water as a transportation highway. Kuzih always found the dock activity interesting, asking many questions about what the boats had transported and where they had come from.

Arriving at the docks, the trio found two riverboats securely moored. A flurry of men unloaded goods from each boat, placing them on the dock. A paddle wheeler waited patiently offshore, needing one of the riverboats to leave before it could come in. Kuzih watched in fascination, amazed at the bustle of activity happening around him. The young boy looked in awe at the different items piled on the dock in front of him; boxes, crates, and machinery, just some of the assortment.

Kuzih enjoyed seeing the teams of oxen and their wagons arriving at the docks to carry the goods to their final destinations. Many of these items were headed to the hotels and saloons in town, as well as other places of business which had ordered merchandise to see them through the winter. After watching for awhile, Kuzih lost interest and wanted to go home. He wanted to check on Daisy and the other animals living in the barn.

Returning to their house, the trio were met by both Rafter and King. The two dogs had quickly established a friendship and enjoyed exploring outdoors together. A cold breeze blew in the faces of the trio, as they went to the barn to visit the animals. Kuzih fed each donkey and Daisy an apple, petting each one. Once done, Wendy took Kuzih to the house, while Jason went to feed the dogs. Entering the kitchen, Wendy added wood to the hot coals of the woodstove to warm the house before dinner. She knew another winter would soon be upon them, and hardships would grip the land as a game of survival began.

CHAPTER
TWENTY-SEVEN

The Gypsy Queen's whistle sounded, as the paddle wheeler and barge's long four-hundred-mile journey from Whitehorse to Dawson would soon be over. The captain of the boat rounded the last corner in the river, before the dock he needed to maneuver into came into view. The captain noticed the wharf was clear of other boats, which made his job easier. It was a formidable task, which only the most experienced operators dared to attempt, successfully navigating a large vessel and a barge loaded with goods into port.

Samuel's brother stood on the bow, watching the men and women congregate on shore. The gathering crowd was waiting for the Gypsy Queen to dock. With little fanfare, and a lot of luck, the captain skillfully landed the Gypsy Queen, maneuvering the large boat and barge gracefully, with no mishaps. Within minutes, the vessels were tied securely to the pier by the men working on the docks. Samuel's barge of merchandise to restock his store had been successfully delivered to Dawson.

One of Samuel's customers came to the store to inform

him the barge loaded with his ironware products was offshore, the captain getting ready to put into dock. Samuel immediately closed his store, heading toward the river. He was excited to see his brother, Dave, but not enthused with the amount of work he was facing. The contents of the barge needed to be moved from the dock, usually under a strict time limit set by the dockmaster.

Samuel greeted his brother with open arms, Dave was exhausted and hungry after his long journey on an uncomfortable boat with minimal creature comforts. The old riverboat was used like a tugboat, pushing barges up or down the river, ferrying passengers an afterthought. Samuel took David to the finest restaurant in town, located in the most exclusive hotel in Dawson. Dave ate his fill of roast beef and potatoes, smothered in gravy.

After eating, the men walked to Samuel's house, where they were greeted by Spearmint, who had stayed home today. Samuel left his brother to nap, while he went to the moving company to arrange the transport of his goods from the barge to the store. The owner of the freight business had heard about the barge of merchandise at the dock and was already preparing to do the job for Samuel. He had organized the men needed for the job, who were preparing the oxen and wagons.

Samuel left the man's business, pleased with his efficiency. His next stop was Wendy and Jason's house, where he asked for Jason's help at the store. Jason told Samuel he would meet him at his business in thirty minutes. Thanking him, Samuel left to walk back to his ironware store, to await his delivery.

CHAPTER
TWENTY-EIGHT

By the time Jason reached the store, two men were unloading a wagon and carrying items inside. Samuel was yelling out orders, telling the workers where to place the merchandise once they carried it in. Samuel's brother, Dave, had awoken from his nap and had joined the work crew unloading the wagons.

After four hours of hard labor, by a total of nine men and six oxen, the job was finished. Six new woodstoves sat in a storage room at the back of the store, four of which were already sold. Samuel earned a healthy profit from each of the stoves sold. Woodstoves were hard to find and a needed commodity when living in the Yukon.

Wendy and Kuzih walked into the store just as the men were getting ready to leave. Wendy looked through the new products and purchased a new kettle and cooking pot for use on top of the woodstove. The new cookware was made from metal which was lighter than those made from cast iron. Jason and his family left the store, followed by Dave and Samuel, who locked the door behind him.

Wendy told Jason they needed to stop and see Luke at the

livery stable, as they needed food for the donkeys and Daisy, the newest resident living in the barn. When they arrived, Luke took Kuzih to see the new donkey he had purchased from a man in a hurry to leave town. The animal's name was Bruno, and he was looking for a permanent home. Kuzih loved donkeys, giving Bruno a hug and pat on his head. Unfortunately for Kuzih, his parents told him he could not take Bruno home, but he could come visit him until Luke found someone in need of a donkey.

Wendy and Jason gathered up their purchases and walked home, where their first stop was the barn. Jason and Kuzih fed the donkeys and Daisy, the always hungry ox. Wendy fed the chickens and checked to see if there were any eggs to gather. As winter approached, Jason would slaughter half of the population of chickens for the outdoor freezer. The baby chickens hatched in the following spring would grow and replace the adult birds Jason had slaughtered for food.

Suddenly an idea popped into Jason's head, fresh chicken for dinner. He decided to catch and slaughter a bird to cook over the campfire tonight. The evening was warm with no wind, an occurrence which was rare as fall was upon them. Wendy took Kuzih to the house while Jason did the dirty deed of catching and killing their dinner. It was a job neither Jason nor Wendy felt guilty doing, as killing an animal for food was an accepted way of life in this not so giving land.

CHAPTER
TWENTY-NINE

Shortly after Wendy and Kuzih left the barn, Jason found a nice plump chicken, which he caught and slaughtered. Before taking the carcass back to the shed to clean and prepare it for cooking, he stopped and started the outdoor fire. Dusk was descending over Wendy and Jason's house, as a light breeze blew across the darkening sky. King and Rafter were following Jason, hoping for a handout while he cleaned the chicken.

Checking the fire, Jason realized the heat from the burning wood would soon be hot enough to cook the chicken. Looking at the woodpile reminded Jason of his own wood problem. Two men from Wendy's tribe would be arriving soon to cut and stack the couple's winter's supply of firewood. This arrangement worked well for both Jason and the Beaver brothers, as Jason did not have to spend endless days harvesting wood and the brothers earned money to purchase essential items.

King and Rafter sat by the campfire, the smell of the chicken cooking over the open flame tantalizing their taste buds. The canines sat licking their chops, waiting for this special dish the dogs would get no share of. Whitefish was on their menu, much to King and Rafter's disappointment.

The stars and moon lit up the night sky, casting their light below. The chicken was sizzling over the fire when Wendy and Kuzih joined Jason and the dogs. The forest surrounding them was quiet, only the occasional sound of an owl hooting breaking the silence. Kuzih sat on Wendy's lap, her mother's warm blanket wrapped around him protecting him from the night air. The couple stared in silence at the night sky, memories flooding their thoughts of days gone past.

Jason stood up to retrieve the whitefish he had purchased in Dawson earlier in the day for his dogs. Calling King and Rafter over to the shed, he fed the canines one whole fish each. This was the preferred way the huskies liked to receive the raw fish. The dogs had favorite parts they liked to eat first.

Rejoining Wendy and his son at the campfire, Jason took the now done chicken and put it on a plate to cool. The dogs had finished their dinner and had returned to the campfire, hoping to be offered some chicken, what the animals really wanted. The family enjoyed their dinner sitting by the fire, ignoring the canines waiting nearby.

Wendy soon retired to the house to put Kuzih to bed. Jason stayed by the fire, with the dogs for company. He let the wood burn down to the coals, enjoying the serenity of the evening before retiring to the house to find Wendy and go to bed. In the morning, Jason was helping his friend, Samuel, organize the goods that recently arrived. Although it was all in the store, it was still cluttered and needed to be put out for display. Samuel expected a large crowd tomorrow, people wanting to look at the new merchandise available for sale. With these last thoughts in mind, Jason drifted off to sleep, dreaming about working at the ironware store tomorrow.

CHAPTER THIRTY

J ason left his house early the following morning. He reached the ironware store at the same time Samuel and his brother, David, arrived. Sam unlocked the door and let the men inside. Spearmint decided he would rather stay home today, ignoring his owner's call to come when Samuel was leaving.

The store was full of new product, left exactly the way it was dropped yesterday from the loaded wagons. To add to the chaos in the store, Samuel decided to open for customers while the men worked to put the merchandise on display. He did not want to lose any chance of a sale, as it was more important than ever for Samuel to liquidate the stock in his store before spring. This was when he planned to leave Dawson, returning to Seattle to live.

The trio worked hard for two hours before the store opened, managing to bring some semblance of order to the store before Samuel opened the doors and let the crowd in to shop. By the end of the day, Samuel had sold the remaining woodstoves, and all the stove pipes he had ordered. The day's sales were good, with Samuel guessing he sold twenty per cent of the stock in his store.

Jason left the ironware store to return home for dinner, while Samuel and Dave stayed to wait for a customer who was returning with a wagon to pick up the stove and pipes he had purchased. On his way home, Jason stopped by the fish peddler to pick up whitefish for his dogs and some trout for him and Wendy for dinner.

Arriving home, Jason was surprised to find they had visitors. Johnathan, Shining Star, and their son, Grey Eagle, had travelled to Dawson to take a break from the monotony of everyday life at their cabin. They had travelled without hurry, stopping at the beautiful lake the couple used as their personal campground on their trips to Dawson. Shining Star and Wendy were cousins, both married to white men who had come to the Yukon seeking their fortune. Johnathan and Shining Star wanted to visit Samuel's Cast Iron Creations before he sold out of his most popular items. They planned to leave their purchases in Wendy and Jason's barn until freeze up, when they could retrieve the items using their dogsled. Johnathan also wanted to talk to Samuel about buying his furs this winter. He had heard the man would pay top dollar for any fur the family and friends of Wendy and Jason brought in.

The day before leaving their home, Johnathan had shot a young doe. The couple had shared some of the raw venison with their neighbours and fellow trappers, Black Hawk and White Dove, who lived a three hour walk from their cabin. Johnathan smoked the remaining meat, not wanting any of it to spoil and go to waste. He had carried the smoked venison to town, the two couples now sharing it for dinner tonight. Wendy and Jason enjoyed the company of her cousin and husband, this was yet another small dose of friendship and feelings of good will in a cruel land where survival, not happiness, was the priority.

CHAPTER THIRTY-ONE

The following morning dawned cloudy and cool; the landscape in the Yukon was changing. The trees, once green during the summer months, were now full of colour. The leaves falling to the ground created a kaleidoscope of beauty which covered the forest floor.

Wendy had risen with the sun, leaving Jason and Kuzih to sleep while she went downstairs to prepare breakfast. After letting King outside, she stoked the hot coals in the woodstove and added fuel. She placed her new kettle on the cooktop, to boil water for coffee. Wendy waited for the oven to get hot, planning on baking some bread to eat with breakfast. The smell of the bread baking in the oven brought three hungry adults to the kitchen table. Pork purchased from a man in Dawson, along with eggs from Wendy's chickens in the barn, was what the friends were sharing for breakfast.

Kuzih and Grey Eagle were the last to come downstairs, their main concern not being hungry, but wanting to find their mothers. The group sat around the kitchen table, enjoying the fine breakfast Wendy prepared. They loved the camaraderie of eating together. When breakfast was finished, Johnathan and Shining Star took the boys with them, as they headed to the barn to feed the animals and to meet Daisy. Kuzih was anxious to show them the ox who had recently been added, along with another dog, to the family. When Johnathan opened the barn door, the group's presence was met by a multitude of sound.

Johnathan fed the happy donkeys, but everyone paid special attention to Daisy, the ox. Kuzih told them Daisy was the strongest animal around, which Grey Eagle believed, as he had never seen such a large, domesticated animal before. Prior to leaving the barn, Grey Eagle and Kuzih fed the donkeys and ox apples, left from harvesting the trees earlier in the fall. After they finished taking care of the animals, they returned to the house.

Johnathan told Wendy he and Shining Star wanted to walk into Dawson to go to the general store and to visit Samuel's ironware store, planning to return before lunch. Wendy told the couple to let Grey Eagle stay behind, so he and Kuzih could play together. She was sure he would have more fun exploring the woods around their house with his cousin than shopping, and knew Johnathan and Shining Star would enjoy not having to drag him to the stores with them.

The cloudy sky had cleared, giving way to sunshine, which warmed the spirit of the couple on their walk to town. They stopped at the general store to purchase commodities such as coffee and sugar, items they could carry on their long trip home to their cabin. They also stopped in at the livery stable and bought two large bags of dried dog food. They informed Luke Jason would be by to collect the bags within the next couple of days.

Samuel greeted Johnathan and Shining Star inside his store, the couple identifying themselves as family of Wendy and Jason. They told him they hoped to buy some useful items, which they would leave at the store for Wendy and Jason to pick up later. Samuel told Johnathan and Shining Star they could enjoy a ten per cent discount on their total purchase.

The couple bought kitchen utensils, an axe and saw for cutting firewood, and an iron poker for stirring the hot coals in their woodstove. Samuel told Johnathan he would buy all of his fur this spring, paying more than the other two buyers in Dawson. The couple also purchased a small amount of candy for Kuzih and Grey Eagle, something they knew the boys would like. Thanking Samuel, the couple walked back to Wendy and Jason's house, happy with their purchases and ready to head back to their cabin in the woods tomorrow.

CHAPTER THIRTY-TWO

As Johnathan and Shining Star walked back to Wendy and Jason's house, they talked about how thankful they were Black Hawk had agreed to stay at their cabin to care for their dogs while they were away. The couples living in the bush often would exchange dog sitting duties with one another, allowing them to get away for a short time each summer. This event was the fur trappers rendition of a summer vacation.

Upon their return to the house, Johnathan and Shining Star saw Jason and Wendy talking to two men by the front door. It was two young men from Wendy's tribe, who had arrived to cut the couple's supply of firewood for the winter. They had arrived with two horses and supplies to last them until they were finished with the job. The two men planned on setting up a teepee for shelter, using a campfire inside to keep warm at night.

Anxious to get started, the Indigenous men planned to set up their camp near a deadfall of trees and cut wood from this area first. They would then move on to the next stand of dead trees, which they would cut down for firewood. The men hoped to finish this job after two weeks of hard work, looking forward to being paid and returning home.

As part of their arrangement, Jason promised to supply these men with food while they were here working on his property. Wendy suggested the outdoor freezer could now be used to preserve food, as the nighttime lows were near or below freezing. The couple decided to take the canoe out this afternoon to catch fish for themselves and the young men here to cut the firewood. Tomorrow, Jason would hunt for a deer he knew had taken up residence nearby. He had been waiting patiently to be able to use his outdoor refrigeration for the first time this season. He was also looking forward to eating fresh venison steak, fried on the woodstove.

Wendy and Jason introduced Jonathan and Shining Star to Little and Big Beaver. The brothers excused themselves, anxious to get their camp set up before nightfall. Johnathan and Jason decided to take the canoe out and try to catch enough fish for everyone for dinner, while Wendy and Shining Star went to harvest some late season vegetables from the garden. Kuzih and Grey Eagle begged to go with their fathers, but were told they had to stay home as there wasn't enough room in the canoe for both them and fish.

As the men approached the water, a wayward beaver far from his habitat let his presence be known by slapping his flat tail against the quiet water of the lake. Johnathan and Jason launched the canoe into the pristine water. After two hours of fishing, the men were up to their ankles in fish, glad they had not allowed their sons to join them. Happy with their catch, they paddled back toward the house. Jason called for Grey Eagle and Kuzih, offering to take them with him to the Beaver brothers' camp to deliver some of the fish for their dinner. Johnathan took the rest of the catch to the shed to clean, placing some of the meat in the outside cooler and taking the rest in the house for their own supper.

CHAPTER THIRTY-THREE

Wendy, Jason, and their company were sitting down to dinner when a knock sounded on the front door. Jason opened the door to a smiling Samuel and Dave on the other side. Jason invited his friend and his brother inside the couple's home. Wendy offered to feed them both, saying there was plenty of food and the more the merrier. The men accepted without a second thought, as Wendy's home-cooked meals were Samuel's favorite.

Over dinner, Samuel asked Jason if he could bring Daisy to the store tomorrow and deliver a woodstove for him. The customer who had purchased the stove lived in town, which meant the job would not take long. Jason agreed, telling him he would meet him at his store at 8 a.m.. He explained Johnathan and Shining Star would be leaving first thing in the morning for their trip back home.

After finishing their meal with a piece of apple pie for dessert, Samuel and David thanked the couple for dinner, leaving to walk home. Wendy and Shining Star quickly cleaned up the kitchen and then everyone left the house to visit the men they had hired to cut their winter firewood.

A short walk brought the family to the men's camp, where Big Beaver and Little Beaver were enjoying the fish Jason had provided to them for dinner. They had cooked the fish over the campfire and were enjoying the succulent fillets.

The men welcomed everyone into their camp, Big Beaver offering the group some bread he had baked and carried with them to Jason's house from their camp deep in the forest. As they had just finished eating, the only ones to take them up on his offer were Kuzih and Grey Eagle, as they always seemed to be hungry. Wendy and Shining Star had brought one of the pies they had made for the brothers to share, a special treat, as apples were not prevalent in the bush.

The group sat around the campfire enjoying the cool northern air. Darkness prevailed as the setting sun threw a shadow over this untamed land. After a long visit, the two parties parted ways. Upon returning to their house, Jason started a fire in the fireplace in the living room. The nights in Dawson were getting colder, meaning more heat was needed to keep this large house warm. Johnathan and Shining Star asked Jason if he would pick up and store their purchases in the barn until the snow came, at which time they would come pick up the goods with their dogsled. Jason said he would be happy to do so after he delivered the stove tomorrow.

The evening was quiet, with only a strong breeze blowing through the remaining leaves of the deciduous trees which made up the forest. The two boys had fallen asleep after coming home from the Beaver brother's camp, exhausted from their busy day. The adults soon followed, the quiet night allowing the couples to sleep peacefully till the first rays of sunlight announced the birth of another day.

CHAPTER
THIRTY-FOUR

The distant sound of a rooster crowing from the barn broke the silence of the early morning. Jason lay in his bed, eyes open, gazing through the bedroom window at the sun rising over the horizon. He pulled himself out of bed, leaving Wendy to sleep. Jason dressed and walked downstairs, where he added wood to the dying coals in the woodstove and let King outside. The month of September would soon be coming to an end, meaning winter would not be long in arriving.

Jason left the house to feed his dogs and then went to the barn to feed the donkeys and Daisy the ox. Today, he was taking Daisy to Samuels's store to deliver a woodstove and stove pipes to a customer in Dawson. Jason returned to the house, to find everyone in the kitchen. He joined them for a cup of coffee and a quick breakfast of bread and jam. Johnathan and Shining Star were almost ready to leave for their long walk home. The couples hugged each other goodbye, wishing each other the best of luck. Johnathan said he would be back once the snow had arrived to pick up the purchases they had made yesterday, however, that would be a solo trip as there was only so much room on the dogsled.

Jason walked out the door with his departing company, watching as they headed for the trail home. He returned to the barn, where he attached a rope to Daisy and led her outside. It was a twenty-minute, uneventful walk to the ironware store. The day was sunny but cold, with a stiff north breeze blowing in Jason's face as he poked along. Daisy was in charge of their motion forward, a slow, steady gait her preferred speed. She moved even slower when pulling a wagon behind her.

Jason arrived at the store and led Daisy around to the back of the building. He hooked up the wagon and had Daisy pull it to the front door. Samuel had arrived at work; the two men loading the woodstove and pipes onto the wagon. Jason sat on the bench seat with reigns in hand, urging Daisy forward. After a fifteen-minute walk through the dusty streets of Dawson, they reached the customer's house. A team of huskies in the back yard barked loudly at Daisy, viewing her as a threat because of her large size.

A man, small in stature, opened the front door and greeted Jason. He introduced himself as Ray, telling Jason he had been successful during the Klondike gold rush. He had decided to stay in the Yukon, purchasing this house in Dawson. Ray told Jason he was happy Samuel had opened his store in town, and was thankful to have been able to purchase the new stove from him.

The men worked together removing the old stove and pipes from Ray's house. Under Jason's guidance, they then installed the new stove, with Ray starting a small fire to make sure it was working smoothy before Jason left. As Jason was leaving, Ray asked him to tell Samuel he would stop by the store later today to pay the balance of his bill. With a wave goodbye, Jason and Daisy headed back to the store.

Jason unhooked the wagon from Daisy, leaving it parked behind the store. He led the ox home to her stall in the barn, and then returned to the house to eat lunch. Although he had originally planned to go hunting today, making the delivery this morning meant the hunt would have to wait until tomorrow. In the meantime, he would scout for deer, as a couple of young men needed to be fed well to perform their duties cutting his winter firewood. He was hoping for a successful hunt tomorrow.

CHAPTER THIRTY-FIVE

Jason told Wendy of his plans this afternoon, scouting for the deer he had seen signs of. Jason had even seen the doe in his yard twice this summer and was fairly sure he knew the animal was living in a thicket of evergreen trees a twenty-minute walk from the house. Jason left with his rifle slung over his shoulder, making King and Rafter stay home, as he feared they would be a liability rather than an asset. Deer were cautious animals and could recognize the scent of a dog from a long distance away.

As Jason approached the thicket, rabbits were plentiful in the meadow, trying to find the last shoots of green vegetation before the snow covered the ground. Jason quietly took up a position where he could watch the area for the deer but not be seen. After a two hour wait, his patience paid off. A mature doe cautiously walked out of the evergreens searching for food to eat in the meadow which fronted the trees where the deer lived. Jason watched the animal, wishing he could shoot her. However, as it was getting late in the day, he knew he would lose daylight before successfully dressing the deer and carrying her back to the house.

He quietly moved from his position, leaving the area.

On the walk home, he shot two rabbits he happened upon, planning to give the rabbits to Big and Little Beaver, the young men cutting firewood. The men could clean and eat the rabbits for dinner tonight. When Jason entered the house, he was met by an enthusiastic son who was glad to see his father. Kuzih jumped into Jason's arms, hugging him tightly around his neck. After embracing his son, Jason set him down, telling Kuzih he would play with him later.

Jason told Wendy he had seen the deer he planned to shoot tomorrow, confident the hunt would be a success. He took the rabbits, which he had gutted in the bush, and placed them in the outdoor freezer for safekeeping. He retrieved Omar from his pen and placed a halter on the donkey. He led Omar to the house, where he scooped Kuzih up in his arms and placed him on the animal's back. Jason told Wendy, who was standing on the porch, he was taking Kuzih and Omar to Samuel's store to buy some candy. Wendy asked Jason to pick her up a stick, as she loved to savor the taste while reading from the book collection which filled the shelves in the living room.

As no rain had fallen on the streets of Dawson for two weeks, Omar's hoofs left a trail of dust behind him as they walked to the store. Upon arriving, they were greeted by Samuel. Kuzih made a beeline for the candy counter, his favorite place in the store. Kuzih picked two hard candies for himself and one piece of stick candy for his mother. Samuel told Jason, his brother, Dave, was returning to Seattle soon. He had booked passage on a boat to take him to Whitehorse. From there, he would continue his travels by train and ship to Seattle, where he owned a home which a relative was taking care of until his return.

Jason placed Kuzih on Omar's back, as Samuel gave the donkey a big hug. He loved the kind, gentle animal like it was his own. On the way back home, Jason stopped at the livery stable to pick up Johnathan's dog food and talk to Luke, the owner. He needed to place a large order for dry food for the dogs, bedding and hay for the livestock, a bag of feed for Wendy's chickens, and bags of grain to feed the donkeys and ox. This order should be enough food to keep his animals from going hungry this winter. Luke promised to deliver the items when they were available.

· Kuzih had been visiting Bruno while his dad was conducting his business. Luke had still not found a buyer for the donkey, of which Kuzih was glad. Jason called his son and placed him back on Omar's back. As they were leaving, Luke stuck a large wild apple in Omar's mouth, which the donkey gracefully accepted. The trio left the stables and walked back home.

Returning Omar to his pen, Jason let Kuzih feed each donkey and Daisy an apple as a treat, something these animals always expected. Jason and his son then walked back to the house, to a waiting Wendy, who was wondering why it had taken them so long to run a simple errand. Jason told Wendy about stopping at the livery stable to order feed for this winter. He told Wendy he was going to retrieve the two rabbits he shot earlier in the day and take them to the Beaver brothers for dinner.

When Jason arrived at the camp, he talked to the men about the deer he was hoping to shoot tomorrow. Jason asked for their help in carrying the meat from the kill site to his shed. The brothers agreed, looking forward to eating venison for the rest of the week. Jason left the brothers' camp and walked back home. He planned on eating dinner, and then going to bed early so he would be well rested and alert for his hunt tomorrow.

Jason was looking forward to putting meat in his freezer for the first time this year. He fell asleep anticipating achieving this goal tomorrow, shooting a deer to provide food for family and friends who depended on him, including Kuzih, his child. The belief that no one would go hungry while he was in charge was Jason's last thought before falling asleep, not waking until the following morning.

CHAPTER THIRTY-SIX

Dark storm clouds filled the morning sky; a light frost covered the barren ground. Jason dressed warmly, as the September morning was cold. He walked downstairs and added wood to the stove. He lit the fireplace in the living room to further warm the house. Jason returned to his wife, who was in bed upstairs, telling her he would be leaving soon to go hunting. Wendy wished Jason luck as he walked out the bedroom door.

Jason gathered up his rifle, ammunition, a knife, and a bone saw. Jason also carried a rope which he planned to use to hang the deer from a tree. He would gut the deer before cutting it into more manageable pieces to carry home. He preferred to butcher the deer in his shed, out of the cold drizzle which had moved into the area. Jason walked the short distance to where the doe was living, and took up a position which provided a good view of his surroundings.

Jason waited for the deer to come out from the cover of the trees. He did not have to wait long. Shortly after Jason arrived, the doe walked out into the open meadow, giving Jason the unobstructed shot he was looking for. He did not hesitate, shooting the deer through the heart with a high caliber bullet, killing the animal instantly.

Walking over to the dead animal lying on the cold ground, Jason stopped briefly to thank the Creator for the food. He threw his rope over a sturdy branch of a nearby tree and pulled the deer over to it. He hoisted the deer up, took out his bowie knife, and gutted the animal. He left the deer hanging in the tree while he walked to the brother's camp to get help moving the animal from the kill site to the shed.

Upon Jason's arrival, the men were happy to hear he had bagged the doe. The brothers grabbed their knives and left with Jason to retrieve the kill and move it to Wendy and Jason's house. After a twenty minute walk, the men arrived to where the deer was hanging. Jason untied the rope, easing the animal to the ground. The men pulled the deer out into an open area and got to work, taking the hide off the animal first. Wendy wanted to keep the deer skin to make a rug to lay in front of the fireplace in the living room.

After skinning the dear, Jason and the Beaver brothers cut it into quarters. They would carry only these quarters to the shed, leaving the waste for the hungry scavengers living in the area. The men each grabbed a quarter of the deer, leaving one for Jason to retrieve later. They walked back to the house and placed the meat in the shed. Jason thanked the men for their help before they returned to resume their work cutting wood.

Jason returned to the house, wanting to share his success with Wendy. Jason asked if she wanted to join him on his return trip to where the deer had been shot, as he needed to pick up the other leg quarter and the hide which had been left there. Jason suggested they take King and Rafter with them, allowing the huskies to eat their fill from the inedible leftovers at the kill site.

The entire family left for the short walk, the dogs running ahead and helping themselves to the pile of discarded waste from the butchered deer. Kuzih wanted the jaw from the deer to add to his collection of odd things he had gathered over the past year. Jason grabbed the rest of the deer meat, Wendy carried the hide, and Kuzih carried the jawbone his father had removed, teeth intact. The group left for home, leaving the huskies to finish eating.

When the couple and their son returned home, Jason carried the meat to the shed, along with the hide from the animal. He then returned to the house to relax and drink coffee before going back out to finish butchering the deer. Jason needed to take some of the meat to the men's camp, where they were cutting wood for him and Wendy. But first, Jason would enjoy some coffee and a piece of pie Wendy had baked when he was out on the hunt this morning. A man's job was never finished when he lived in this land called the Yukon, Canada's proud land in the north.

CHAPTER
THIRTY-SEVEN

J ason finished his coffee and pie before returning to the shed to finish butchering the deer. King and Rafter waited outside the shed door, taking turns catching scraps of deer meat Jason threw to them. Jason cut the meat into smaller pieces appropriate for cooking or smoking later. After he finished, he stored the majority of the venison in his outdoor freezer, keeping enough meat out to feed his hired help and for his family's dinner tonight. Jason also kept out a nice piece of meat to give to Samuel and his brother, David.

Returning to the house, Jason told Wendy he was walking to the Beaver brothers' camp to give them the venison he had promised. Then he was going to walk into Dawson to give Samuel and his brother some meat for their dinner tonight. Jason left, soon arriving at the campsite of Little and Big Beaver.

Jason took note of the large stack of small to medium-sized logs, ready to be moved to his house. When the men surmised they had cut enough trees for the winter, Jason would borrow a wagon from Samuel, which Daisy could pull to the woodpile. The wood cutters would haul the timber back to Jason and Wendy's house, where the logs would be cut into smaller pieces and split to fit into the woodstove. Some larger pieces of wood would be left to fuel the fireplace in the living room.

Giving the brothers the meat and telling them they were doing well, Jason said good-bye to the men and continued to his next destination. Seeing Jason, Samuel welcomed him into the store with a handshake and a big hug. Jason gave Samuel the venison, which made the store owner happy. He told Jason, Dave had just mentioned to him how he wished he could enjoy a venison dinner before returning home to Seattle. Samuel said his brother would be pleasantly surprised to have this wish fulfilled. Jason left Samuel's store, heading home to his wife and child.

Samuel and Spearmint spent the entire day at the store, keeping it open late, hoping for customers to stop in and purchase the inventory he needed to liquidate. He hoped his stock would be gone by late spring or early summer, Samuel's target date for moving back to Seattle.

Near dusk, a man came into the store carrying a small number of furs on his back. He had traded a rifle to an Indigenous man for the fur. Samuel examined the hides the man had in his possession, finding the fur to be in fine condition, with no visible damage. Samuel checked his price list, the amount he could pay for each type of fur, and made an offer, which the man accepted. Samuel paid the man, both parties happy with the deal that was made.

Samuel waited for another thirty minutes to see if another customer would show up. But when no one else came, Samuel gathered up his dog and the package of venison Jason had gifted him and walked home. Dave was waiting for Samuel, pleasantly surprised when he returned with the venison Jason had given them. Sam, being the more experienced cook of the two, fried the deer meat on the hot cooktop of the woodstove. Spearmint enjoyed sharing the three pounds of venison the men ate for dinner.

David would be leaving Dawson soon, as he had booked passage for the first of October. This would be the start of a long journey home. Samuel told David about his plan to sell his store, land, and house next summer and join him in Seattle in the fall. This was a secret only the two brothers shared, Samuel telling no one else. David was sorry to hear Sam's plans to stay in the north hadn't worked out, but was thrilled at the prospect of having his brother living close by again.

The men were finishing dinner when there was a knock at the door. It was a man who lived in Dawson, who was carrying two valuable beaver pelts. He had shot the animals in the head while they were working to strengthen their dam for winter. The man had processed the animals, keeping the meat and looking to sell the pelts.

The man had stopped by Samuel's store and read the sign informing anyone with fur to come to the house if the store was closed. Samuel had left directions on how to reach his home, knowing anyone with pelts could easily go to one of his competitors. Sam did not want to take a chance on losing prospective customers of his fledgling brokerage business.

Samuel purchased the beaver pelts, the stranger walking away from the house happy. Samuel was surprised at the good start his fur buying business was seeing. Word was already out among the local trappers, Samuel was an honest man who paid above average prices for fur. He respected the hard-working men and women trying to make a living trapping in the secluded wilderness of Canada's north. These folk displayed courage and a respect for nature, necessary prerequisites for surviving in this savage land.

CHAPTER
THIRTY-EIGHT

Once the after-hours customer left, the two brothers sat around the kitchen table discussing David's departure, as he was leaving to return to Seattle in a few days. David had a reservation to depart on a riverboat the first of October, which would take him to Whitehorse. From there he would take the train to Skagway, Alaska, where he would board another ship to take him home to Seattle.

The nights in Dawson were becoming colder as the late September weather spread across the desolate land. The snows of winter would soon arrive, covering this frozen wilderness in a coat of white. A strong north wind rattled the windows of Samuel's house. He was glad he had ordered a supply of wood from local woodcutters, who had delivered and piled his winter supply on his porch, beside the front door of his house.

David was happy he was leaving for Seattle soon. He had no intention of staying in Dawson, a frontier town where it was not uncommon to find temperatures dropping to forty degrees below zero during the winter. The night sky was black, except for the countless stars shining down on this near barren land. Spearmint lay by the woodstove sleeping, the dog's loud snoring could be heard throughout the small house. Samuel and his brother played cards till the men's eyes became heavy and wanted sleep. The next few days passed quickly, and soon it was time for Dave to embark on his journey to Seattle.

Three days later, in the early morning, the brothers headed for the waiting riverboat David would be boarding for Whitehorse. Jason, Wendy, and their son, Kuzih, were meeting them at the dock to wish Dave farewell and a safe journey home. The paddle wheeler loomed large over the dock, as columns of black smoke rose from the ship's smokestack. The boat was preparing to leave Dawson on it's voyage to Whitehorse.

The friends arrived at the dock at the same time. Kuzih was intrigued by the large vessel, wanting to go aboard. The captain, being a nice man, allowed Kuzih to walk the gangplank with him, escorting him to the wheelhouse. He let the child turn the wheel, making him think he was piloting the large craft. After answering several of the child's questions, the captain returned a happy Kuzih to his parents.

The boat's whistle blew, giving the paying passengers a ten-minute warning before departure. David hugged everyone goodbye, knowing he may never see Wendy and Jason again and it would be months before reuniting with his brother. With tears in his eyes, David boarded the ship and found a spot to stand by the railing.

As the boat left the dock, it gave two short blasts with its whistle. A sense of melancholy swept over both parties, as they watched the riverboat round a bend in the river and disappear out of sight. Wendy and Jason invited Samuel to come to their house for breakfast, which he graciously accepted. Sam never turned down a chance to eat Wendy's home cooking or enjoy Jason's hospitality.

CHAPTER
THIRTY-NINE

S amuel was quiet while eating breakfast with Wendy and Jason. His thoughts were with his brother, now on his way home after spending the previous two weeks with him. Samuel also thought about his friendship with Wendy and Jason. Their short relationship had blossomed into what would be a lifelong connection for both the couple and Samuel. The thought of saying goodbye to Wendy and Jason when he left Dawson next summer, made his heart ache. Leaving Dawson was not a pleasant thought Samuel liked to think about, although he knew returning to Seattle was the right choice for him.

The month of October passed quickly. The winds of change transformed the once green oasis into a sea of brown vegetation. The once barren land, now covered in snow, marched on toward the month of November. Samuel sold all the woodstoves and pipes he had in stock, liquidating them from the store's inventory by the third week of October. They had all been sold locally, the buyers transporting them to their homes. This allowed Jason to avoid a job he did not particularly like performing and gave Daisy a well-deserved rest.

The water on the area's wilderness lakes was forming a layer of ice. The waterfowl, which called the Yukon home in the summer, were on their winter vacations, the birds needing to find open water for their survival. The birds would return in mid-April, depending on when the warmer weather arrived in Dawson.

Wendy and Jason asked Samuel if he would move into their home for a few days at the end of November. They wanted to both attend the annual moose hunt held for the extended family of fur trappers living in the bush. This important event was intended to secure meat for these families' outdoor freezers for the winter. Samuel agreed to take care of all the animals, including King, who would stay with Spearmint, his favorite company.

By the first week of December all boat activity on the Yukon River came to a halt. Ice covered the water, making it impossible for such vessels to continue any kind of commerce. In two weeks, this vast body of water would be frozen, making the ice safe to move supplies by dogsled. Mushers from remote wilderness traplines would use the river as an expressway, a superhighway for the dogs pulling sleds to Dawson to cash in their valuable furs.

Samuel planned to close his ironware store while he looked after Jason and Wendy's house and animals. However, not wanting to miss out on any business, he would leave a notice on both the front and back doors explaining where he could be found. With a promise of moose meat for his freezer, Samuel was ready to do this favor for his best friends in Dawson, one he knew would be returned many times over by the couple he regarded as family.

CHAPTER FORTY

The grey November sky cast a dark shadow over the spirits of the people living in Dawson. The men and women residing in this desolate town knew they would soon have the ravages of a cruel winter unleashed upon them.

Business at the ironware store was slow, with few customers visiting unless the weather was favorable outside. Samuel's business purchasing fur was doing well, with most of his customers being Indigenous trappers. These men traded their fur for cash, but were also interested in bartering for merchandise from his store.

One sunny day in mid November, Samuel was surprised when an Indigenous woman, leading a horse laden with goods, entered his business. She had fur, blankets crafted by her late mother, a deerskin rug, and numerous hand-crafted items representing various aspects of her culture. She introduced herself as White Feather, saying she had been born and raised in the wilderness of the Yukon.

The young woman told Samuel she was trying to raise enough money to purchase a cabin in the bush for herself and her future husband. She was selling her late mother's personal belongings, which she had inherited when her mother passed away less than a year ago. White Feather felt she could part with these with her mother's blessing, knowing the money would be spent on a cabin for herself and Sky Eagle. In a dream, White Feather's mother had appeared to her, telling her to sell her worldly items, giving her approval of her daughter's upcoming marriage and future plans. She had already stopped at a few proprietors in town, who did not want to deal with an Indigenous woman.

Samuel bought all the items White Feather had carried with her, thinking he would take them to Seattle where their value as collectible native artifacts would be greater than trying to sell them locally. Upon leaving, Samuel told White Feather he would purchase more fur and other similar hand-crafted items from her in the future. White Feather left Samuel's store feeling a friendship built on trust was developing between them.

One morning late in November, Samuel answered a knock at his front door. Spearmint was already standing by the door, tail wagging, as he knew who was behind it. A welcome greeting was given to Wendy, Jason, and Kuzih as they entered Samuel's home. Jason wanted to invite Samuel to go with them to the docks at the river. Wendy and Jason wanted to take Kuzih to watch for dogsleds arriving loaded with furs remote trappers were bringing to Dawson to sell.

Standing on the dock looking down the river, the group watched as one dogsled came racing up the frozen water toward them. The musher was yelling commands to his team and the dogs were barking, announcing their arrival.

Kuzih pointed in awe as the trapper, dressed in fur, and his dogsled, loaded with the fruits of his labour, swept past them on their way into town. Kuzih told his parents he wanted to be just like that man some day.

CHAPTER FORTY-ONE

An icy wind blew off the frozen river, slamming into the exposed faces of the people standing on the dock. Kuzih shook from being cold, prompting Wendy to tell Jason they needed to leave for home soon. Wendy asked Samuel if he would like to come back to their house for a visit and a cup of coffee. Samuel agreed, never turning down an invitation to visit with Jason and Wendy. This couple were the only true friends Samuel had in town.

After a short walk, the group reached Wendy and Jason's house. Wendy added fuel to the woodstove, whose coals had burned down to ashes. Jason started a fire in the fireplace in the living room, to allow more heat to circulate through the big house. Within a brief time, the kitchen was warm.

While sitting around the kitchen table, Samuel asked Jason if he would be able to take some furs to a Hudson's Bay trading post to sell for him. Samuel was running out of cash, which was needed to buy hides from the men and women who came with fur to sell. The trading post was a one-day round trip by dogsled. Jason agreed to do this job when they returned from the moose hunt. With that thought in mind,

Samuel left Wendy and Jason's house, returning home to his faithful companion, Spearmint.

After arriving home, Samuel lunched on some smoked fish Jason had given him today, sharing the fish with Spearmint. When finished eating, the duo prepared to go to the store, as Sam wanted to open for business. Upon arriving, he placed his "open" sign in the window. Directly below that, was another sign which read, "If door is locked, check the shed at back of building". This afternoon, the shed was exactly where Sam planned to work, sorting furs.

Samuel was busy examining furs and placing like ones together, when he was startled by the loud braying of an unhappy donkey. The donkey was hungry and tired from carrying a heavy load on his back, five miles through the bush to Dawson. The trapper accompanying this animal was broke and needed money to purchase food for himself and his animals.

Samuel looked over the furs Charlie had brought to town. The hides were of good quality, and Sam especially liked the wolf pelt which was among them. Samuel knew Steward had an affinity for wolf skins, as members of his tribe used the hides for ceremonial purposes at Indigenous events. Sam and Charlie agreed upon a price for the furs, with the trapper and his donkey leaving happy with the cash they had been paid.

Samuel decided to give the wolf hide to Steward, and would ask Jason to take it to him when he attended the moose hunt in a few days. The wolf was sacred to the native people, its spirit being a part of the Yukon since life began.

CHAPTER FORTY-TWO

Wendy, Jason, and Kuzih were preparing to leave their home in Dawson to travel to Steward and Blossom's cabin. The family moose hunt was an annual event, held in various locations in the bush. This year Steward was hosting, as the land surrounding his property was ideal moose habitat, virtually guaranteeing the hunters their prize.

Samuel had arrived at Wendy and Jason's house early this morning. Over breakfast, the trio conversed freely about the couple's upcoming trip to Steward's cabin. Sam wanted to review what was expected of him while the couple were gone. When finished with breakfast, Jason left the house and hooked up his dogs to his sled. As both Wendy and Kuzih were joining him this year, he attached a small sled behind his larger one. This is where he would carry the wolf pelt Samuel was gifting to Steward, and where he would place the meat from the hunt for the return trip home.

Jason mushed his huskies to the front of his house, where he and Wendy finished loading their belongings they needed for this journey. With Kuzih wrapped in a heavy blanket, Wendy and Jason wished Samuel goodbye, as they started their trek to Steward's cabin. Samuel waved at the departing dogsled as it moved down the trail, into the forest, and out of sight.

Silence fell over the property with Wendy and Jason's departure. Samuel walked back to the house with King and Rafter in tow. He added firewood to the embers in the woodstove and sat for a brief time in the comfortable living room. Samuel decided to leave King and Rafter sleeping by the stove while he walked into Dawson. He wanted to stop at his house to pick up Spearmint and then head to the store.

The day was sunny but cold. By the time Samuel arrived at his store, a man was waiting for him. The man's dog team and sled were parked at the front of the store. The trapper's dogs were anxious and noisy, not pleased with being forced to wait for their owner to complete his business. Samuel told the man to bring his dogsled to the back of the building, and he would meet him there.

Jacque was a French-Canadian, who had moved to the Yukon from Quebec twenty years ago. He ran a trapline in a pristine area, its location known by no one else. The oasis was a perfect habitat for prime fur trapping, Jacque keeping its whereabouts a well guarded secret. Samuel examined the furs Jacque had brought to him, and ended up purchasing the pelts of two beaver, a lynx, and a wolverine. Jacque told Samuel this was just a sampling of the fur he processed at his cabin. Samuel paid a premium for the furs, with Jacque promising he would return with more in the future.

Samuel stayed at the store until the late afternoon. He only had one other customer all day, who bought a set of tools for his fireplace. Samuel locked up his store an hour before dusk, leaving Spearmint there for the night. He needed to return to Jason's and Wendy's house, where he was staying. He still had to feed the animals in the barn and collect the eggs from the chicken coup. With that thought in mind, Samuel walked off into the beginning twilight, planning to enjoy the company of the animals, who were now his only visible friends.

CHAPTER FORTY-THREE

After locking up the store, Samuel returned to Wendy and Jason's house. Upon his arrival, he walked directly to the barn. Opening the door, Samuel was greeted by a chorus of animal sounds. He fed the donkeys first, showing them affection by rubbing their heads and backs. Samuel then walked over to visit Daisy, his ox he boarded at Jason and Wendy's barn. After feeding the large bovine and spending time talking to her, Sam rubbed the ox's head affectionately before moving on to the chicken coop. There, he fed the cackling birds and collected six eggs from the nesting boxes. Finished with the chores in the barn, Samuel returned to the house, to a waiting King and Rafter.

The dogs greeted Samuel at the door, where he let them out to use the bathroom before he fed them dinner. Samuel relit the woodstove and fireplace, whose fires had burned out. Within a short time, the house warmed, allowing Samuel to remove his heavy clothing and lay on the couch in the living room. A loud bark and scratching at the door by King, meant the dogs wanted back inside. Sam rose from his comfortable position, letting the dogs in and feeding them dinner.

Three days passed with no sign of Wendy and Jason. But on the fourth afternoon, Samuel was sitting in the kitchen drinking coffee when he heard dogs barking. King ran to the door first, knowing Wendy, Jason, and Kuzih were soon going to be home. Samuel went to open the front door of the house and was greeted by a smiling Wendy and Jason, with a sled full of moose meat and venison.

Jason, Wendy, and Kuzih entered the warm house, following Samuel to the kitchen. He made coffee for the couple, who appreciated the hot drink after their long, cold dogsled ride home. Kuzih had acquired a taste for coffee on the trip, preferring to drink the liquid with lots of sugar. After a brief visit and short rest, Jason and Samuel went outside to get the moose and deer meat into the outdoor freezer. Wendy had already brought the couple's personal belongings indoors and put them in their rightful places.

After unloading the meat from the sled, Jason settled his dogs into their yard, feeding them before returning to the house. Samuel was anxious to get to his store and collect Spearmint. While Wendy and Jason were at Steward's cabin, Samuel had spent most days at his store, accompanied by his dog. Earlier today, he had left Spearmint lying beside a nice warm fire in his fur shed, a smaller area to heat than the main store.

Wendy and Jason thanked Samuel for looking after their home and animals while they were away. Jason gave his friend ten pounds of moose meat, which Sam readily accepted. He hugged Wendy and Jason goodbye, leaving to get Spearmint, who by now would surely be hungry and longing for Samuel's company.

CHAPTER FORTY-FOUR

Samuel was buying large amounts of fur. Word was out in the community, he was an honest man who paid top dollar for the valuable furs brought by local trappers and natives who lived in the area. He was known to never turn away a hungry trapper, buying fur, even if in deplorable condition, to allow the starving man to eat. The inventory in Sam's Cast Iron Creations store was slowly disappearing, as he sold one or two pieces of merchandise a day. Customers were always asking him what he had planned for the spring; what new products he would be carrying in the store.

One day in mid-December, two men came into Sam's fur shed, who he instantly felt were up to no good. The ruffians told Samuel they were there to offer him a deal, as one of them handed Samuel a canvas bag. In the bag were six bottles of liquor, the worst nightmare for the Indigenous population. Called firewater by the locals, the liquor was detrimental to the native community. The men told Samuel they were out of money and running from the law. They wanted to sell the alcohol to him, telling him he could trade it to native trappers for their fur; one bottle could demand many furs from an addicted Indigenous trapper.

Spearmint, growling from his place by the woodstove, caught Samuel's attention. He looked at Spearmint and gave the order to chase the two men from his fur shed. The dog, growling and snarling, sprang toward the men, baring his teeth. Samuel quickly grabbed his loaded rifle, pointing it at the duo as they headed out the door. He couldn't help but laugh as Spearmint caught the seat of one man's trousers, almost ripping his pants off his body. Samuel yelled at Spearmint to release his prey and return to the fur shed. Sam praised his dog, congratulating him on a job well done.

Samuel immediately locked up the store and fur shed to walk to the North West Mounted Police Station. He wanted to report the two men, whom apparently the Mounties were looking for. At the time, it was illegal to sell or trade liquor to anyone in the Indigenous community. Samuel would like to see these men caught and sent to jail. The constable thanked Samuel for the tip, telling him he would send a couple of his men out to look for the pair.

When Samuel left the Mountie's headquarters, he walked straight to Jason and Wendy's house. After his encounter with the strangers in his shed, he was uncomfortable leaving his valuable haul of furs guarded only by a flimsy door, which could be knocked open with one hard kick. He wanted to ask Jason if he could take the furs down the frozen Yukon River to the Hudson's Bay trading post soon. Samuel was also short on cash and expected an influx of fur to come into his store before Christmas.

After a short walk, Samuel and Spearmint reached Jason and Wendy's home. Rafter met Spearmint at the front door, barking to let Jason know they had company. Samuel was hoping to receive the answer from Jason he was looking for.

CHAPTER FORTY-FIVE

Jason invited Samuel inside, the men joining Wendy in the kitchen for coffee and hot rolls and butter. Samuel told the couple he and Spearmint had enjoyed a delicious dinner last night of fried moose meat, cooked to perfection on the woodstove. He then related the story of his encounter with the two men in the fur shed, and explained the reason for his visit. He needed a musher and a dogsled to carry a load of furs to the Hudson's Bay post, located four hours upriver. Small trading posts had been set up by the Hudson's Bay Company to purchase furs from the wilderness and Indigenous trappers throughout the territory. Samuel asked Jason if he could do this task for him.

With a warm smile and a nod from his wife, Jason accepted the offer. He felt his huskies would love the daylong run in the fresh open air of the Yukon wilderness. The friends finished their coffee, with Jason saying he could leave at dawn tomorrow to deliver Samuel's furs to the trading post. Arrangements were made for the two parties to meet at the fur shed at the back of Samuel's store shortly after daybreak. Jason was excited about going on this trip with his sled dogs.

That night, Jason did not sleep well, tossing and turning in his bed all night unable to get comfortable. The anticipation of tomorrow's events kept him awake most of the night. The first rays of the sun cast a faint light through the bedroom window. Jason pulled himself out of bed, dressed, and went downstairs to the kitchen. He let the dogs outside and grabbed the bag of jerky he had prepared the night before. The jerky was what he planned on eating for the entire trip.

Jason called King and Rafter back inside the house, before leaving to pick up his dogsled. Jason hooked up the small sled behind the larger one.. He would carry frozen fish on the small sled, to feed his dog team when they reached the trading post. This would recharge the dogs' batteries for the four-hour trip home.

Within twenty minutes, Jason left his house and was on his way to Samuel's store. Upon Jason's arrival, Samuel, with his dog Spearmint, were waiting by the front door of the shed. Jason mushed his dog team to the doorway. After pleasantries were exchanged, the men loaded the bales of fur on the dogsled. With the load secured, Jason shook hands with Samuel, saying he hoped to see him before dark. With a yell from Jason, the dog team shot forward in the direction of the river. The long journey to the Hudson's Bay trading post was about to begin.

CHAPTER FORTY-SIX

Within minutes, Jason's sled was moving down the frozen, snow-covered Yukon River. His huskies, moving at breakneck speed, left a cloud of white behind them as the runners of the sled sliced through the soft snow. Jason slowed his dog team down to a fast trot. He did not want his dogs to tire quickly, as they had a long journey ahead of them.

The day was sunny, but cold. Jason had dressed warmly, knowing the wind against his face would be icy. Wendy had crafted Jason a covering for his face made from muskrat fur. She had sewn it into the hood of Jason's parka to help keep his face warm when travelling by dogsled.

The river was quiet, only the panting dogs broke the silence of the wilderness which surrounded Jason and his dogsled. Two hours into the trip to the trading outpost, Jason had only passed two other dogsleds heading in the opposite direction, both mushers driving their dog teams toward Dawson. In the distance, Jason saw smoke from a trapper's cabin drifting aimlessly through the treeline by the riverbank. Before reaching their destination, traffic picked up on this Yukon highway, as dogsleds loaded with fur became a common sight the closer Jason got to the trading post.

After a four-hour uneventful trip, Jason and his dog team arrived at their destination. A chaotic situation surrounded them. Hungry dogs, left unattended too long by their owners, displayed aggression toward other canines nearby. Jason pulled his sled up to the building, where men working for Hudson's Bay secured his furs. He then parked his sled and took care of his dogs. When finished, Jason returned to the building, lining up behind two men who had arrived before him wanting to sell their furs.

When it was his turn, the broker examined Samuel's furs. The man told Jason the pelts were of fine quality, and he could pay a premium for the cache of furs. Jason accepted the broker's offer and was paid in cash. Jason left the trading post, knowing Samuel would be happy with the deal he had made. Having fed his dog team the fish he had carried here before seeing the broker, the dogs were now rested and ready to go home.

Jason left the outpost happy with the results of selling Sam's fur. Two hours after leaving, the trip home became quiet; only the panting of the sled dogs could be heard breaking the pristine silence. Jason saw movement on the frozen river ahead of him. As the dog sled drew closer, Jason saw a pack of wolves eating a deer the predators had chased onto the river and killed. He clutched his rifle closely and mushed his dogs toward the kill sight. The wolves were eating and not paying attention to their surroundings, allowing Jason to move closer to his prey. Three shots rang out in succession. Jason waited to see the results of his actions, hoping to see a dead wolf when the smoke cleared.

CHAPTER
FORTY-SEVEN

After the gunshots rang out, there was complete silence. Two wolves lay dead in the blood-stained snow, while the remaining wolves had escaped the bullets and run off into the forest. Jason moved his dogs closer to the kill site. He disembarked from his sled, examining the wolves he had shot. He quickly gutted the animals and positioned their bodies on the secondary sled he was pulling. He would take them back to Dawson, knowing wolf hides were selling for a premium, as the fur had become quite popular in Europe.

A hind quarter of the deer had been untouched by the wolves. Jason had the tools to cut the meat from the deer and take it home for his freezer. After an hour of work, the deceased wolves and deer meat were loaded and secured on the sleds. Jason mushed his dog team towards the middle of the river and continued his journey home.

The afternoon was waning as Jason rounded the last corner of the river before the buildings in Dawson came into view. A short time later, he was leaving the river and mushing the dogs to Samuel's store. Jason wanted to unload the wolf carcasses into Samuel's shed before heading home to his wife and son, Kuzih. Samuel was still at the store, waiting for Jason to return.

Samuel was happy to hear the journey had been successful, as Jason gave him the money Hudson's Bay had paid for the furs. After counting the cash, Samuel paid Jason fifteen per-cent of the sale, thanking him for a job well-done. Sam also purchased the two dead wolves, with Jason telling Samuel he would return tomorrow to show him how to prepare the hides for sale.

Jason left Samuel's store after dark to return home, mushing his dogs into the front yard. Wendy had heard the team approaching and was waiting at the front door with Kuzih, and their two dogs, King and Rafter. They greeted Jason, with the couple embracing and Kuzih tugging on his father's pant legs, wanting to be picked up. Even the two dogs were glad to see Jason, jumping up on him and giving him big wet kisses.

After the excitement calmed down, Jason took the deer meat and placed it in the shed. He would process the hindquarter tomorrow and store the finished product in the outdoor freezer. Jason then returned his dogs to their yard, fed them frozen whitefish, and provided unlimited water to drink. Finishing his work outside, Jason returned to a warm house and wife. Wendy was preparing dinner when Jason walked into the kitchen, his stomach growling. He had not eaten anything but jerky since leaving on his trip down the Yukon River.

The couple enjoyed being back together as a family. Wendy always worried when Jason left, thinking he might never make it back home safely. This was their reality living in this realm of wilderness not meant for man, where nature rules and death can happen quickly and unexpectedly.

CHAPTER
FORTY-EIGHT

Wendy and Jason lay awake in their bed, eyes open. After eating dinner, the couple had retired to the living room where they read books from the library. Wendy had continued using the library after Bev's passing, when they took possession of the property. The couple found reading helped keep their minds alert, avoiding a slowdown of body and spirit brought on by the isolation of living in the Yukon.

A full moon shone brightly in the dark sky, a million shining stars illuminating the night. Wendy and Jason fell into a peaceful slumber, not waking until a barking dog downstairs alerted the couple to a knock at their front door. Jason quickly got dressed and walked downstairs to answer the knock. King and Rafter stood silently by the door, tails wagging, wondering who was visiting their house this early in the morning.

Jason opened his front door to a smiling Luke, the owner of the livery stable in Dawson. King and Rafter greeted Luke before running out the door past him. Jason invited the man inside, Luke saying he needed a favor from Jason. An old prospector, who had worn out his welcome in the bush, had arrived at Luke's livery stable yesterday with a near frozen, hungry donkey. He told Luke he could no longer care for Lucy and was willing to sell her at a deeply discounted price. Feeling sorry for Lucy, Luke purchased the donkey from the man, immediately taking the donkey inside, feeding her, and giving her fresh straw to sleep on.

Luke told Jason his problem was he had no extra room for Lucy to stay with him. Luke said he had a full house, with all the animals people brought for him to board over the winter. By this time, Wendy and Kuzih had joined Jason and Luke in the kitchen. Wendy had heard the last of the conversation between the two men and knew what Luke was going to say next. Luke asked Wendy and Jason if the couple could board Lucy in their spacious barn for the entirety of the winter. Wendy and Jason were happy to help their friend; Lucy would have a warm, dry place in the couple's barn until the spring.

Luke left Wendy and Jason's house a happy man, telling the couple he would bring Lucy to their barn after lunch. After Luke left, Wendy placed some bread in the oven to bake and cooked eggs she had gathered from her hen house in the barn for breakfast. After eating, the trio, with Kuzih in the lead, went to the barn to feed the animals and prepare a stall for Lucy, the newest addition to the family of animals in the barn.

Upon opening the barn door, the group was met by a chorus of barnyard noises, a pleasant greeting from the animals who lived there. Kuzih played with the donkeys, while Wendy and Jason fed them hay from Luke's stable. The group then fed and watered Daisy, the resident ox, who also lived in the barn, and prepared a pen for Lucy beside the other donkeys' living quarters.

CHAPTER FORTY-NINE

The mid-December day was cold in Dawson. After finishing their work in the barn, Wendy, Jason, and Kuzih returned to their house. The temperature outside prompted Jason to add more firewood to the woodstove. The couple were sitting in their kitchen drinking coffee when they heard an approaching dog team. King and Rafter ran, waiting by the door, always glad to see company. Wendy and Jason walked to the front door, wondering who was outside.

When Jason opened the door, a smiling Grey Wolf and Rose, with their dog Nicky, greeted him. After a warm welcome was expressed between the two couples, Wendy invited them inside, out of the cold winter air, happy to see her distant cousin and her husband. She served everyone hot coffee and rolls she had been baking in the oven. Sitting around the kitchen table, Grey Wolf told Jason and Wendy they had come to Dawson to conduct some business. In the winter months, trapping at their wilderness cabin was the only life this couple knew, making them happy to have an excuse to break the monotony.

Grey Wolf wanted to see Samuel, as they had carried fur

they had trapped to Dawson to sell. Grey Wolf also wanted to purchase a small sled from the ironware store to attach behind his dogsled. He hoped Samuel still had this piece of equipment for sale. The sled would be useful in moving meat from a kill site, hauling traps for the trapline, and transporting fur when needed.

Over coffee, the couple talked about the upcoming Christmas party Wendy and Jason were hosting. Wendy told Rose, Grey Wolf and she were welcome to help pick this year's Christmas tree, a tradition they were planning on undertaking with Kuzih tomorrow. Rose happily accepted Wendy's invitation to join them on the hunt for the holiday tree.

The couple left Nicky to play with King and Rafter while they traveled by dogsled to Samuel's store. When they arrived, they found Sam at his store with his dog Spearmint, who was sleeping comfortably by the woodstove. Samuel reached out to Grey Wolf and Rose, hugging them both in greeting. He purchased the fur the couple had carried with them from their cabin in the bush. Grey Wolf was lucky to buy the last sled Samuel had in stock. He had ordered ten sleds from the foundry in Portland and had already sold nine. As Grey Wolf and Rose were leaving, Samuel told the couple he would see them at Wendy and Jason's house at Christmastime, as he would be joining the family for dinner.

On the way back to the Wendy and Jason's house, Grey Wolf and Rose stopped at the general store for a few staples and then the livery stable for dry dog food. Arriving back at the house, they noticed activity at the barn. While they were gone, Luke had brought Lucy from his stable to her new home at Wendy and Jason's. When Lucy entered the barn, she was welcomed with a chorus of greetings from the other farm animals who lived there. This lucky donkey could have it no better.

CHAPTER FIFTY

The mid-December night was cold, a howling wind rattled the bedroom windows keeping Grey Wolf and Rose from getting a peaceful night's sleep. The rising sun broke through the clouds which covered the sky, throwing its early morning rays of light through the bedroom windows. Grey Wolf and Rose pulled themselves out of bed and dressed. The couple walked downstairs to join Wendy and Jason in the kitchen for breakfast. Minutes later, Kuzih wandered into the kitchen still half asleep. He climbed onto Wendy's lap, snuggling into his mother's arms. Wendy hugged Kuzih tightly, the little boy falling back asleep.

Jason finished preparing breakfast while Wendy took Kuzih upstairs to get him dressed. A brief time later, they returned to the kitchen and rejoined the group. Everyone sat down and ate breakfast together. After finishing this early morning meal, the two couples and Kuzih were heading to a wooded area behind the house to cut a Christmas tree. Dressing warmly, the group gathered up the family dogs and, with axe in hand, left the house.

The dogs bounded toward the woods, cutting a trail through the deep snow for the others to follow. The skies had cleared, the bright sun causing the white snow surrounding the group to sparkle like twinkling stars. After examining several trees, Kuzih picked the evergreen he liked best, with a little help from his parents. With a few blows of the axe, the tree lay in the snow. With Kuzih's help, Grey Wolf pulled the Christmas tree back to Wendy and Jason's house, with the family dogs again leading the way.

Arriving back at the house, Grey Wolf stood the tree against the wall on the porch, while Wendy and Jason prepared the area in the living room where the Christmas tree would stand. After lunch they would place the tree in the living room and decorate it. In the meantime, Wendy boiled a kettle of water on the cooktop of the woodstove. The two couples sat around the kitchen table drinking hot coffee while Kuzih played with the dogs.

Barking sled dogs caught Jason's attention, followed by a knock at the door. It was Luke from the livery stable, returning with a bag of feed for Lucy, the donkey he had brought to Wendy and Jason's barn the day before. Jason followed Luke to the barn, where he fed the animals belonging to him and Wendy, while Luke took care of Lucy. After finishing these chores, the men returned to the house for conversation over coffee in the kitchen.

Thirty minutes later, Luke headed back to town, to continue a job he had been working on at his livery stable. The streets of Dawson were empty, the cold winter air keeping everyone in their homes where it was warm. Meanwhile, Samuel was getting ready to lock up his store and head to Wendy and Jason's house to decorate the Christmas tree.

Jason and Wendy had invited Samuel to take part in this holiday tradition a week ago. Samuel had said he would not miss this opportunity, joining his only friends in Dawson, who were like family to him.

CHAPTER FIFTY-ONE

Jason retrieved the Christmas decorations he had taken from the attic earlier, placing them by the evergreen tree the group had put up in the living room after eating lunch. Kuzih waited patiently for the tree decorating to begin. A knock at Wendy and Jason's front door meant Samuel had arrived. He was invited into the house and greeted with hugs and kind words from the people inside.

Kuzih liked Samuel, wanting him to pick him up and carry him around the house. Samuel pulled some candy he had carried with him from his store from his pocket. He gave the candy to Kuzih, who like most kids enjoyed the tantalizing treats. Samuel had also brought his dog with him, and had left Spearmint outside to hang out with the other dogs present at Wendy and Jason's home. Sudden barking from the animals outside announced the arrival of yet another visitor.

Jason went to the front door and watched as a dogsled, driven by a Mountie, pulled up to the front of the house. He was carrying a load of venison to store in Jason and Wendy's outside freezer. No one in Dawson went hungry at Christmas time, as Wendy and Jason distributed meat to the downtrodden during the holidays. Such charitable work had been performed yearly by Bev, Wendy's aunt, who was the previous owner of their home. Jason and Wendy had inherited the house after Bev's death, promising her they would continue her caring demeanour during the Christmas season.

Jason showed George, the constable who was a recent transfer from Edmonton, where the outdoor freezer was located. With little fanfare, the men unloaded the deer meat from the dogsled, with George telling Jason he would be returning with another load before Christmas. With those last words, the Mountie returned to his post, while Jason returned to an impatient Kuzih, who was waiting to decorate the tree.

While everyone in the household worked on trimming the tree, Jason decided to return to the attic for a box of decorations he was missing. He must have overlooked them when he removed the other boxes from the space last week. Jason had purchased a metal stepladder from Samuel, who had ordered six of these folding ladders, all of which sold immediately. Jason used his new ladder and climbed from it into the attic, lighting the lantern kept there. The small window at one end of the space did not provide enough light to move about freely.

Jason took the lantern and looked for the box of missing decorations. He called for Grey Wolf to come and retrieve the found box, which Jason had somehow missed. He passed the box to Grey Wolf through the trap door in the ceiling. Jason decided to take a last look around the attic before returning to the living room.

He looked at the sled Bev's father had built when she was still a child. Bev had not wanted the sled ruined, storing it in the attic for safekeeping. While inspecting the quality of the workmanship, Jason noticed something unusual under the sled. A small metal box was concealed under the blanket the sled sat on. Jason retrieved the box, planning on opening it when he returned to the living room. He climbed down the ladder, replacing the hatch in its proper place in the ceiling. The box in his hand was a mystery, which would soon be solved.

CHAPTER FIFTY-TWO

Jason left the attic and upon his return to the living room, the tree decorating stopped as the focus fell upon the box he was holding. He told the group of curious onlookers about examining the sled Bev's father had built and finding the box under the blanket the sled sat on. The occupants in the house gathered around Jason, waiting to see what was inside the container he held. Opening the lid revealed something unexpected, a mummified finger with its nail still attached. A feeling of shock spread through the observers of this anomaly.

Wendy knew the story of the finger, as Bev had shared her father had severed his finger by accident while butchering a moose years ago. The sharp knife he was using had slipped unexpectedly, severing his finger. This was all Bev had ever told her about this story, never disclosing the mummified remains of the finger were hidden in her attic.

After a lengthy conversation, Jason headed upstairs to return the appendage to where he had found it, vowing to leave it alone forever, not touching or moving it again. After doing so, he returned to the living room to help finish decorating the tree. Jason picked up Kuzih, instructing him to place the angel on the crown of the tree. Reaching up to the top, he placed the angel where his father had told him. This act completed the decorating of the Christmas tree until other guests who were coming for the holidays would add personal mementos of their own to the evergreen's branches.

Wendy headed to the kitchen with Kuzih and Rose in tow. She planned on making bread dough and baking sweet rolls for dinner. Wendy already had a large moose roast in the oven, with Samuel staying to join them for the evening meal. The men took Kuzih and headed for the barn to visit the animals, planning to shower the donkeys and Daisy with affection, before letting Kuzih gather the eggs from the chickens. When they returned to the house, the smell of the baking bread overwhelmed their senses upon entering.

The rest of the afternoon was whittled away with inactivity by the men, while they waited for the women to finish preparing dinner. The holiday season was almost upon them, with Christmas morning being only a week away. Grey Wolf and Rose would leave tomorrow for home, but would return to Jason and Wendy's for the annual Christmas celebration.

Soon, Wendy called everyone to dinner, flushing the hungry men from the living room to the kitchen to enjoy their meal. After eating the delicious food the women had prepared, Samuel gathered Spearmint and left to return home. He had eaten too much, making himself tired and somewhat listless. He was looking forward to lying down in the comfort of his own bed and staying there for the remainder of the night, a restful sleep was what Samuel longed for.

CHAPTER FIFTY-THREE

The following morning after breakfast, Grey Wolf and Rose left Wendy and Jason's house for their return trip home. They packed their dogsled with their belongings, not forgetting the items they had bought from Samuel's ironware store. The couple wished Wendy and Jason goodbye, telling them they would see them in a week for Christmas. Shortly after leaving with their dog, Nicky, Grey Wolf and Rose passed George, the Mountie, who was delivering another load of meat to Wendy and Jason's outdoor freezer.

The day was sunny, but cold. The dogs pulled the sled purposefully through the soft snow toward the young couple's cabin. Grey Wolf and Rose's trip home was uneventful, and they soon found themselves pulling up in front of their homestead. After unloading the sled, Grey Wolf took care of the dogs, while Rose lit a fire in the woodstove to warm the cabin, which was as cold as the air outside. The wind picked up, and soon dense cloud cover spread over the land.

Grey Wolf returned to the cabin, telling Rose they needed to prepare for a blizzard. He headed to the outside freezer to retrieve two packages of moose meat and extra fish for the dogs to eat. Rose carried in a supply of firewood for the woodstove. Before going to Wendy and Jason's house, the couple had pulled all their traps from their trapline, not planning on resetting them until they returned from Dawson after Christmas.

While the couple ate dinner, the wind grew stronger. The lower branches of the large hardwood tree which hung over the cabin scraped against the roof, distracting Nicky as she tried to sleep by the woodstove. Grey Wolf thought when the storm was over, he should trim some of the limbs off the tree to avoid this annoying noise in the future. The fury of the blizzard struck in the early evening, the small cabin providing safety, ensuring they would not die in the storm.

The wind continued to blow hard all night, keeping Grey Wolf and Rose from getting a peaceful night's sleep. When the couple awoke the following morning, a ray of early morning sunlight shone through the cabin's windows. The blizzard had ended during the night, leaving a veil of new white snow covering the trees and the landscape.

Grey Wolf dressed, opening the cabin door for Nicky to go outside. Shortly afterwards, he followed Nicky to check on the sled dogs. The animals were fine, but hungry. Grey Wolf retrieved some fish from the outdoor freezer, feeding them breakfast. He then returned to the cabin, letting Nicky back inside the building. Returning to bed, Grey Wolf snuggled with Rose under the warm blankets her mother had made them.

The following week passed quickly and soon Christmas was upon them. The couple had prepared the items they were taking to Dawson early in the week, and were now loading them on the small extra sled they had purchased from Samuel. This provided enough room for Nicky to ride on the sled if she became too tired to keep up with the sled dogs.

Grey Wolf locked up the cabin and he and Rose left on their trip to Dawson. The weather was pleasant and the dogs were ambitious, pulling the couple to town in record time. Nearing Wendy and Jason's home, the couple noticed other dog teams tethered near the house. After Grey Wolf parked his sled and secured his dogs, he and Rose, with Nicky in tow, walked to the house to join their friends and family for Christmas.

CHAPTER FIFTY-FOUR

G rey Wolf's knock at the door was met by a smiling Wendy, who graciously invited the couple into her home. They left Nicky outside to play with the other families' pets, who were attending the Christmas celebration with their owners. Grey Wolf and Rose were the last couple to arrive, joining four other fur trapping couples who also lived in the bush.

Jason, seeing Grey Wolf and Rose, walked over to greet them, leading the young couple to the kitchen table where a generous amount of Steward's smoked fish was set out on a platter, ready to be eaten. The couple fixed themselves a plate of succulent trout, along with a serving of hot bread fresh from the oven. This year, Wendy had decided to have the main dinner on Christmas Day instead of the night before. Bev, the previous hostess of this family tradition, had had the large dinner on Christmas Eve, so her siblings could attend. Bev's two sisters had liked to spend Christmas Day with their adult children in Dawson, but loved seeing everyone in Bev's family the evening before.

These three Indigenous sisters had all passed away within one year of each other, leaving Wendy now in charge of these gatherings and able to make her own decisions regarding the scheduling and menu. After the smoked fish had been consumed, the platter was refilled with large helpings of venison and moose meat for guests to eat whenever they were hungry. The afternoon soon turned into evening, with the night sky absent of clouds and a light breeze blowing across the frozen land. A bright moon shone down on Wendy and Jason's house, a beacon of light and hope for the men and women who called the Yukon home.

The outside of the property was a beautiful sight to behold in the moonlight. The sled dogs were sleeping peacefully in the snow, while a wolverine had snuck onto the porch of Jason's house, his nose attracted to the meat inside. The noise and commotion inside had deterred King, Rafter, and the other families' pets from catching wind of the unwanted visitor. Once the wolverine smelled the dogs inside, he quickly vacated the premises.

Wendy called everyone into the living room, as she had an announcement to make. When everyone was settled into their places, Wendy told the curious onlookers she was pregnant. A chorus of well wishes announced their happiness at this news. Jason, who was not aware of this precious secret Wendy had kept from him, hugged his wife tightly, crying on her shoulder, expressing his feelings at this beautiful moment.

After the excitement settled down, it was time to hang the mementos the trappers' families had made to celebrate Christmas. Traditionally each made one ornament to hang on the Christmas tree, typically hand-crafted from items found in the forests surrounding their homes. These works of art were placed on the tree in remembrance of Bev and her husband. As they hung them, memories were shared among the men and women who called this wild and untamed land home, memories which would endure in their hearts forever.

CHAPTER FIFTY-FIVE

Wendy and Jason's home was an oasis of peace in a chaotic land. After placing the last mementos on the Christmas tree, Wendy and Shining Star took their children, Kuzih and Grey Eagle, upstairs to bed. Shortly thereafter, the remaining group in the living room retired to their respective sleeping areas, gathering up their dogs to sleep near them. A brief time later, a hush fell over the house, except for the sound of a snoring dog, who was disturbing the silence. The night had turned black, as thick cloud cover had moved into the Dawson area. The howl of a lonely wolf looking for his soulmate was the only other sound to break the quiet of the night.

The dawn sky was grey, with snow flurries filling the sky. Wendy was awake first, letting the waiting dogs outside to perform their morning ritual. She then added fuel to the woodstove and restarted the fireplace in the living room, resulting in warmth spreading throughout the house. The smell of breakfast cooking brought her company to the kitchen area. Wendy, with Blossom's help, shooed all newcomers from the kitchen into the living room to wait for breakfast. Eggs, freshly baked bread, and fried venison were on the menu.

The spirit of Christmas filled Wendy and Jason's house with joy, as family and friends celebrated this special day together. After a lively breakfast, the men in the house joined their dogs outside. They fed their respective teams, as well as the donkeys, ox, and chickens living in the barn. The outside air was cold and blustery, willing the men back into Jason and Wendy's warm dwelling. Upon their return, the women were just finishing cleaning up from breakfast.

The entire group adjourned to the living room for coffee and to open gifts, with Kuzih and Grey Eagle receiving the most presents. An unwritten rule was one gift per adult, names having been picked from a hat the evening of the previous Christmas. The men then socialized in the living room while their wives prepared Christmas dinner. A Canada goose was the main course, with venison and moose being secondary choices of protein. This meat would be supplemented by potatoes and carrots from Wendy's root cellar, which she had grown in her garden and saved for this special occasion. Fresh baked bread and apple pie finished the menu.

A knock at the front door meant company; Samuel, who owned the ironware store in Dawson, had been invited to join his friends on Christmas Day. Wendy and Jason knew he would enjoy the company and the food. The couple felt strongly no one in Dawson should go hungry any day, which is why they offered their outdoor freezers to store meat which was dispersed to the hungry and poor in Dawson over the holidays. Dinner was enjoyed by all, as a feeling of peace swept over the Yukon, memories were made by this wilderness community which would not be easily forgotten.

CHAPTER FIFTY-SIX

The morning after Christmas, the friends and relatives of Jason and Wendy left for their return trips back to their cabins, carrying the fond memories of this year's celebration with them. The Yukon day started bright and sunny, as Steward and Blossom were the last to depart. Steward's dogs ran fast with their heads down, the canines pulling hard on their harnesses, as the huskies knew they were going home. The dogs were looking forward to the familiarity of their surroundings at their cabin, and the food and care provided to them by Steward and Blossom.

Unfortunately for the couple, their trip home was sidetracked by bad weather. Two hours into the couple's journey, the weather soured on them. Dark storm clouds filled the northern sky and a brisk north wind began to blow; the atmosphere was predicting snow. Steward told Blossom there was a shelter fifteen minutes away from their location and they should head for it so they would not get caught outside in a storm. This shelter was one of many built by the North West Mounted Police for the constables to use when performing duties in the bush. The buildings ccould also be utilized by wayward travellers caught in bad weather and needing emergency shelter.

Steward mushed the dogs to the shelter, the strong wind driving the heavy snow which was falling from the sky. Whirlwinds of snow blew around the small building as it came into view. Steward and Blossom entered the shelter. Inside was a woodstove, with a supply of dry wood stacked beside it; a small bed sat in one corner of the room. Steward decided to stay the night, telling Blossom it was too risky for them to travel home because of prevailing weather conditions.

The couple unloaded their belongings from the sled and Steward secured his dogs for the evening before joining his wife in the cabin. Together, the couple lit a fire in the woodstove, which soon made the shelter cozy and warm. The remainder of the day and evening passed quickly, the storm getting weaker before nightfall. Blossom and Steward lay in bed, the blackness of the night pressing around them.

By midnight, the snow had stopped and the sky had cleared, revealing shiny stars glistening in the dark sky. The occasional hoot from an owl hunting for food was the only sound to be heard coming from the quiet forest. The morning dawned with good travelling conditions, allowing the couple to leave the shelter at daybreak. They were anxious to get home as soon as possible to feed their hungry dogs.

Steward did not push his dogs hard, knowing they had not eaten, arriving home during the mid-afternoon. The trip from the shelter had been uneventful and actually pleasant, with the absence of the cold northern wind blowing. Steward and Blossom's cabin in the bush was a welcome sight to the couple, who were glad their trip was over and most happy to be home.

CHAPTER FIFTY-SEVEN

The Yukon winter showed its wrath during the month of January; blistering winds and relentless blizzards gripped the lonely and forgotten land. The people of Dawson waited for spring to return, when life would be reborn. Jason opened his eyes to bright sunshine cascading in through the bedroom window. He wrapped his arms around Wendy, who lay sleeping beside him. He pulled her close, enjoying the love he felt for his wife and their second child.

The winter had been difficult for their friend Samuel. His sanity had been tested, making Wendy and Jason realize this was not a life he could continue. The couple expected him to leave Dawson for good this summer. The calendar had just changed to the month of April, with a steady trickle of trappers coming to Dawson to sell their bounty of furs. Wendy and Jason, who had not seen any of their family and friends who trapped and lived in cabins in the bush since Christmas, were anxious for them to come to town. Soon it would be a race to finish the trapping season, needing to travel to Dawson before the snow melted, making their dogsleds inoperable.

As the season progressed toward summer, Samuel visited

Wendy and Jason to give them the news the couple had been expecting. He was closing his store and joining his brother in Seattle, where life was easier. He hugged Wendy and Jason, sobbing, even though he knew he was making the right choice for his own sanity. The couple were shocked when he offered to give his properties to them, knowing they would make the right decision regarding their future use. Samuel left on a riverboat, *The Little Princess*, two days later, never to be seen in Dawson again.

A new chapter would unfold in the lives of Wendy and Jason, as they continued their struggle called life in this wilderness, a land belonging to the Creator and the strong of heart, a land known as Canada's Yukon.

CHAPTER FIFTY-EIGHT

The recently married White Feather and Sky Eagle had been looking for a wilderness cabin they could call their own. Having been told by a tribal elder he knew of a couple in Dawson who may be able to help in their search, White Feather and Sky Eagle travelled to see Wendy and Jason. When their friend, Samuel, had left the area, he had gifted his properties to the couple. Their good friends, Joe and Mary, after years of fighting the elements while living in the woods had decided to accept Wendy and Jason's offer to move into Sam's home in Dawson, leaving their cabin in the bush vacant. Joe and Mary had agreed to give their old home to a deserving couple, allowing Wendy and Jason to decide who the lucky recipients would be.

White Feather and Sky Eagle were sitting in Wendy and Jason's living room, discussing Joe and Mary's cabin over a cup of coffee and fresh baked bread from Wendy's oven. Joe and Mary had made an even trade with Wendy and Jason regarding the exchange of their properties. The couple had decided to leave their trapping equipment and canoe for the next tenants, only taking their personal possessions when they left the bush and moved into town. Wendy and

Jason, always wanting to help recently married Indigenous couples, offered the cabin to White Feather and Sky Eagle, free of charge. The jubilant couple could not have been more thankful for Wendy and Jason's generosity.

White Feather found it interesting they were being given this gift because the man who ran the ironware store had shared his good fortune with Wendy and Jason. She remembered dealing with Samuel last November, and thought about how kind he had been when he purchased the items she was selling. Sky Eagle told Jason they would return to the their village to pack and pick up their personal belongings, and would return to Jason and Wendy's house in two days. Joe would then take them to their new home in the bush, showing the young couple the cabin and surrounding area.

Two days later, White Feather and Sky Eagle returned to Dawson in the morning, with two horses ladened down with their personal belongings. Jason went into town to summon Joe, who was waiting for the couple's arrival. Joe would accompany them on the three hour walk from Dawson to their new home in the bush. Joe and Mary were happy Wendy and Jason had found the newlywed couple to live in their old home.

Jason returned with Joe, who met White Feather and Sky Eagle for the first time. An instant camaraderie formed between Joe, the young couple, and their dog, Bounty. The dog was a fine husky, gifted to Sky Eagle by his father when the couple married. The group said goodbye to Wendy and Jason, leaving Dawson to walk to their new home. On their journey, Joe shared his story with the young couple, explaining he had returned to the area after living in Seattle for a few years. This was where he had met Mary, who was originally from Europe, and they had married and moved north, as her family was not pleased she had fallen in love with an Indigenous man.

Joe told the couple he and Mary had been given the cabin by an old trapper, who was not in good health and unable to stay living in isolation any longer. He had been a friend of Wendy's aunt, and had been desperate for someone to take care of his dog, who he could not take with him to Seattle. Leonard, the trapper, had offered Joe and Mary his cabin if they promised to look after Rusty, his beloved dog. It was a generous gift, which had turned out better than expected for Mary and him. However, Mary had found life in the bush difficult and was happy to be living in the city. Joe felt comfortable with the decision to move into town, where he could work as a chimney sweep and mason, in addition to taking over Samuel's fur brokerage business.

The day was sunny and warm, allowing the trio to arrive at their destination just after noon. Joe removed the extra security from the front door, and entered the cabin, noting everything looked the same as when he and Mary had left. White Feather and Sky Eagle were thrilled with their new home, the cabin being better than they had envisioned. Joe gave the couple a detailed tour of the property, including the outbuildings, outdoor freezer, and the lake. He suggested they keep the horses in the fur shed overnight, before returning them to their village, as wolves in the area might attack the animals.

Before beginning his walk home, Joe told the couple

to please visit whenever they were in Dawson. An ecstatic White Feather and Sky Eagle waved goodbye to Joe as he disappeared into the bush, leaving the couple alone. A glimpse into the future now looked bright, with their new cabin in the forefront. The couple and their dog, Bounty, walked into their home and shut the door, their new life as an independent, young married couple was about to begin.

CHAPTER FIFTY-NINE

A whinnying sound coming from outside reminded the couple they needed to unload their belongings from the horses. They opened the cabin door, letting Bounty out first. The dog had been waiting patiently to explore and mark his new territory. White Feather and Sky Eagle happily gathered their personal possessions, placing them in their rightful places in their new home. The couple then took the horses to a nearby meadow, where the animals grazed until their stomachs were full. The happy couple then returned the horses to the fur shed, a secure building which would keep the animals safe from predators. Bears and wolves would consider the horses delectable treats not often found in the forest.

The late June sky was vivid blue in colour, with a gentle, warm breeze. The day was deceptive, as the true nature of living in this harsh, but beautiful, land overwhelmed the young couple. They were aware of the challenges they faced living alone in a cabin in the wilderness. With no fear and trust in their Creator, they believed their lives would prosper and grow.

A bark from Bounty, the family dog, caught the couple's

attention. They followed the barking until they found Bounty, under a tree. Sitting on an upper branch, looking down on the dog, was a young porcupine, who had been born in the spring. Showing no fear, the prickly animal was antagonizing the canine, making White Feather and Sky Eagle laugh at this encounter in the forest. Eventually, they told Bounty to leave this harmless creature alone and come home.

The trio walked back to their cabin, where a quick glimpse of an animal running under the structure caught the couple's attention. Investigating, they discovered a burrow, surmising it belonged to a fox who was living under their new home. They decided to name the animal Charlie, a suitable name for either a male or female.

Bounty bounded over to where the couple was standing, wondering what White Feather and Sky Eagle were talking about. Upon seeing the burrow, the curious dog started digging toward the fox's home, throwing dirt into a pile behind him. The couple left Bounty to satisfy his curiosity, which they hoped would result in him leaving the fox and its den alone in the future.

White Feather and Sky Eagle returned to their cabin to have a nap. When they awakened, they took stock of what was in their cabin, pleased to find most everything needed for everyday life. Later they walked to the lake to enjoy the sunset together. The life White Feather and Sky Eagle desired was beginning in a positive way, setting them off on a wilderness journey they would not be denied.

CHAPTER SIXTY

The first rays broke over the horizon, the warm sun bathing the faces of White Feather and Sky Eagle in light as the couple lay motionless in their comfortable bed. Sky Eagle pulled himself out of bed to let Bounty, who was waiting at the front door, outside. Upon opening the door, Bounty spotted Charlie, the resident fox, out in the grass. Like a bullet, the dog shot out the door, running towards small animal. The fox scooted back into the safety of his den, leaving Bounty looking bewildered unsure of what to do next.

Sky Eagle shut the cabin door, leaving the dog to his own doings. The couple ate a breakfast of smoked fish, the last of the food they had in the house. Today they planned to take the horses, which had been locked in the fur shed overnight, to their village. With breakfast finished, the couple gathered up their horses from the shed and, with their dog Bounty, left on the three hour walk to town.

The journey with the horses was uneventful, the couple soon found themselves at Wendy and Jason's home in Dawson. Wendy and Jason were glad to see White Feather and Sky Eagle, inviting them in. The couple enjoyed coffee and Wendy's oven baked bread, a delicious treat anytime of the day or night. After a brief, restful visit, White Feather and Sky Eagle left the couple's house and continued on their way. It was another two hours of walking to their destination, an Indigenous camp deep in the forest.

A pleasant surprise awaited the couple on the trail, as Bounty, who was always off exploring the surrounding woods, began barking loudly. Sky Eagle knew his dog was chasing a larger animal through the woods. The couple stopped the horses, waiting to see what Bounty was chasing toward them.

Sky Eagle stood with his rifle ready, when within moments a young deer ran from the cover of the trees, with Bounty in hot pursuit. Sky Eagle raised his gun, shooting and killing the young doe with one shot. The couple praised Bounty for his success in driving the deer into their path. Bounty hovered over the dead animal, tail wagging, knowing he would be treated to a delicious dinner later.

Sky Eagle secured the deer on one of the horses and the couple continued the now short distance to their destination. Upon arrival, White Feather's father and Sky Eagle's parents greeted them. The couple would stay in camp tonight with their parents; the deer the couple carried with them would be butchered and cooked for dinner. There would be a celebration of the couple's independence from the tribe, with everyone enjoying dinner and a party in their honour. The entire village was proud of these young people for making a life of their own, living only on what nature had to offer. With these thoughts in mind, Sky Eagle and his father worked together butchering the deer, a gift provided from the forest, for dinner.

CHAPTER SIXTY-ONE

The smell of cooking venison filled the air, the delicious aroma drifting through the village reminded the people present their hunger would soon be satisfied. This food from White Feather and Sky Eagle was a gift from nature, which would ensure the survival of these native people living in the pristine wilderness. They had not yet been affected by the sins of white men, a people who would destroy their native culture. Eventually, their identity and land would be stolen, changing their way of life and their special relationship with nature forever.

A sense of togetherness spread through the tribe, as they filled their hungry stomachs with the offering of food nature had provided. The celebratory feast went on past midnight, with dancing and drumming dominating the sounds throughout the surrounding forest.

The following morning, White Feather and Sky Eagle prepared to leave the village, saying goodbye to their family who surrounded them. They left with the love and understanding which defined the culture of these natives who lived in the forest with only their Creator to protect them. The two hour walk to Wendy and Jason's house was uneventful. Upon arrival, Wendy fed the couple and their always hungry dog, Bounty. Jason was in town working with Joe, renovating the now empty ironware store into a center where Indigenous people could gather and discuss the ways their people could adapt to the white man's way of life which was being forced upon them.

After lunch and a brief visit, White Feather and Sky Eagle left on the three hour walk home. The couple would not make it to their destination. Two white men, with no moral character, accosted them on the trail. Drunk on whiskey and their anger fueled by the liquor, the men's hatred for this young Indigenous couple was magnified. Sky Eagle had no time to protect himself or his wife from the hateful men, who ambushed the couple, shooting them and leaving their dead bodies where they fell. Bounty, in a state of confusion, ran off into the forest never to be seen again.

This act of hatred was the beginning of the end for the family of fur trappers who called the Yukon wilderness home. They were never able to accept what happened to White Feather and Sky Eagle, destroying their peaceful lives forever. Some members left their isolated homes and retreated further into the wilderness, rejoining their ancestral tribes, believing there was safety in numbers. Others, continued living among the white men, assimilating into their new reality, losing part of their identity for years to come. It was a sad ending to their happy story, two innocent lives taken by two men who had evil in their hearts, never realizing how many others their act of violence would greatly impact.

ACKNOWLEDGEMENTS

M any thanks to my wife, Ruth Ann, and my family for their continued support and help in seeing this book come to fruition.

Printed in the United States
by Baker & Taylor Publisher Services